ANIMAL INSTINCTS

The guards and driver were shouting curse after curse at the animals, but to no avail. Eventually, they had to just accept the inevitable and turn to face what was coming. When they got a look at what was behind them, they dropped from the horses' backs and hit the ground running.

Their eyes went wide as saucers when they saw Clint bearing down on them like a one-man stampede. The guards fumbled at their holsters only to find them empty. The driver started to run in one direction, but quickly turned and ran toward the hill instead.

Watching the three men scramble like chickens with their heads lopped off, Clint couldn't help but find the scene amusing. He hated to admit it, but the way the trio tripped over themselves and their horses to sprint for a hill that was still the better part of a mile away was just funny. He didn't allow those thoughts to be reflected on his face, however. Instead, he wore a mask of pure stone.

His eyes went cold and his lips parted slightly to bare his teeth like the animal he was pretending to be.

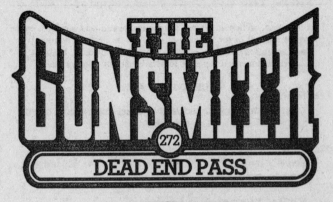

THE GUNSMITH

272

DEAD END PASS

J. R. ROBERTS

JOVE BOOKS, NEW YORK

This is a work of fiction. Names, characters, places, and incidents either are the product of the author's imagination or are used fictitiously, and any resemblance to actual persons living or dead, business establishments, events, or locales is entirely coincidental.

DEAD END PASS

A Jove Book / published by arrangement with
the author

PRINTING HISTORY
Jove edition / August 2004

ISBN: 0-515-13796-0

A JOVE BOOK®
Jove Books are published by The Berkley Publishing Group, a division of Penguin Group (USA) Inc., 375 Hudson Street, New York, New York 10014. JOVE and the "J" design are trademarks belonging to Penguin Group (USA) Inc.

PRINTED IN THE UNITED STATES OF AMERICA

10 9 8 7 6 5 4 3 2 1

ONE

It should have been an easy job; nothing more than a milk run to any but the greenest of hired hands. The job should have been an easy paycheck for an easier couple days' work. It was one of those jobs that got turned down a lot by those with experience and dreaded by those without it. Just a simple delivery from one town to the other was all it was.

It didn't pay much, but there was no reason for anyone to expect it to. Delivery boys didn't get rich until they owned their own companies. When that happened, they could afford to hire their own workers, who would get bored quickly and stop caring about sticking to schedules or keeping every last crate intact.

If it had been a more serious job, laziness would have been a problem. For this job, on the other hand, laziness was expected. All that was required was for the hired hands to stay awake enough so that they didn't fall from their seats during the ride through the central part of Arizona.

Sometimes, even that was too much to ask.

"For Christ's sake, Mikey, watch yerself!"

The driver of the flatbed wagon had to shout to be

heard over the rumble of the wheels as they were pulled over the dry ground by a team of four horses. He was a large man with a salt-and-pepper beard that covered the majority of his face like a fur rug. As he hollered at the man sitting next to him, he took one hand off the reins and used it to smack the other guy's shoulder.

Jumping at the impact of the driver's hand, the younger man shook his head and got a tighter grip on the shotgun in his hands. He was obviously much younger than the driver and was slightly smaller as well. His skin was tanned from the sun and sprouting whiskers that matched the blond color of his hair. Compared to the rich darkness of his skin, the stubble seemed downright odd.

"Jesus, Frank," the younger man snarled. "You shouldn't startle a man with a shotgun like that."

Frank took hold of the reins with both hands again, but leaned to one side so he could nudge the other man with the toe of his boot. "Real tough talk from a kid that goes to sleep like a baby being rocked in his crib."

"Go to hell, old man," the young man said while shaking his head. "I was just resting my eyes."

"Oh, I get it. Then what was that sound I heard a minute ago, Mikey? Either it was you snoring or one of the horses has a damn nasty cough. How about it?" Frank said to the horses. "Any of you coughing or are you sawing logs without me noticing?"

Mikey gave Frank a kick that was a little harder than the one he'd received and then he sat up straight. "I said go to hell. I'm plenty awake."

Content that he'd stirred up his partner enough for the moment, Frank laughed to himself and gave it a rest. Truth be told, he was giving the younger man a hard time to keep himself awake. His own eyes were aching to be closed and his bones were aching to feel a soft bed beneath them for a change.

"How about we head into the next town we see?" Mikey asked.

"The next town we see is the one this load is bound for and it's another day's ride away."

"Then steer for another town. I don't care which one, but there's a few closer than Green Leaf. All I want is a saloon and some women. After looking at nothing but open land and four horses' asses for the past couple of days, I'm about to go out of my mind."

"First you do the job at hand, kid, then you worry about the finer things. You want a saloon? There's a bottle of whiskey behind you. You want a woman? Put that shotgun down and say hello to the only two ladies in this state who haven't slapped that ugly face of yours yet."

Mikey tensed his jaw and said, "I was wrong. I've been forced to stare at five horses' asses this whole time."

Frank looked over at the younger man as though he didn't quite know what to say. Mostly, that was because Mikey didn't say much that was worth listening to. This time, however, Frank doubled up in laughter until he could feel the sting of tears in his eyes.

"Aw, hell, Mikey. That was so funny I'm actually glad I kept myself from pushing you over the side earlier."

Mikey was laughing also after hearing the hearty guffaws that were coming from behind the older man's beard. "Yeah, that sure is . . ." Pausing for a moment after Frank's last words had a chance to sink in, Mikey shifted to look at the other man. "Wait a minute. What did you say?"

Frank didn't respond right away. At first, it seemed that he didn't want to upset his partner. His eyes were riveted to the trail ahead and his fingers clenched tightly around the reins.

"You're kidding, right?" Mikey asked.

After another couple seconds passed without a response from the older man, Mikey's hesitant smile began to fade. "Frank. You were kidding, weren't you?"

"Shut up, Mikey."

"Well, dammit that's just rude!"

"Shut yer damn mouth and use yer head for something worthwhile for a change! You got eyes don't ya?"

"Yeah, and they see better than yours, old man."

"Then how come you haven't seen them?" Frank asked, pointing ahead toward the one o'clock position.

An annoyed grumble was already forming in the back of Mikey's throat when he turned his head to look where Frank was pointing. That grumble stuck right where it was once he saw what Frank had been talking about.

He could definitely tell there were riders coming toward the wagon. The silhouettes were unmistakable.

"How many do you see?" Mikey asked as he checked to make sure his shotgun was loaded. "I make out three or so."

Frank was squinting so much that his eyes looked like slits. "There's three all right. Three across, anyway. They're riding in rows."

"Holy shit," Mikey said, knowing better than to doubt the old man's keen eyesight. "What do you think they want?"

Frank didn't have to answer that question. The gunshot that came from the riders said more than enough.

TWO

Frank had ridden on what should have been much more dangerous runs. He'd driven Wells Fargo payrolls and even rode shotgun on more than one gold shipment and lived to tell the tale with only a scratch or two to show for it. Even as his reflexes took over at the sound of the gunshot, his mind still couldn't wrap itself around what was happening.

Actually, he knew all too well what was going on. It was the why that was giving him so much trouble.

As for Mikey, he was lucky the trembling in his fingers hadn't let the shotgun slip from his hands just yet.

"Slow down," Mikey said. "Bring this thing to a stop."

"What? Are you crazy? We've already been shot at once!"

As if to accentuate what the older man had just said, another shot rang through the air. This time, the men on the wagon could hear the hiss of lead speeding past them as well as the crackle of several more follow-up shots.

Mikey's eyes were wide and sweat was pouring down his face despite the chill in the air. His fists were clenched so tightly around the shotgun that his knuckles had turned white. "I said slow this thing down before the horses get

spooked! Those men'll probably just ride off once they
see we're only carrying a load of timber and building
supplies."

"You may be willing to make that bet, but I sure as
hell ain't!"

"Why would anyone want to rob us?"

"I don't know. Now either you can sit there and cry
about it or you can lift that shotgun and do what you were
paid to do!"

Frank's words were like a splash of cold water in
Mikey's face. Even though he still wasn't settled down
all the way, he knew that talking any more would be
pointless. It was plain to see that the older man meant to
make a run for it and had even brought the horses nearly
to a full run.

With the trail and sky rushing past him and the wagon
jostling beneath him, Mikey turned back to face the oncoming riders. He thumbed back the hammers of the shotgun and lifted the weapon to his shoulder so he could
sight down the barrel. Even though the riders were still a
bit out of range for the scattergun, Mikey took a shot at
them anyhow. The roar of the gun eclipsed the pops of
the riders' pistols, making the young man feel a little better.

Now that they were closing in, Mikey could see that
Frank had indeed been right. The riders had been traveling
in rows of three—three rows of three to be more precise.
As they swarmed closer and closer, the riders kept firing
their weapons at the wagon. They were shouting something to one another as well, but Mikey couldn't hear what
was being said. In fact, he couldn't hear much at all after
he emptied the shotgun's second barrel.

The ringing in his ears only added more to the chaos
that had dropped upon them like a storm. He reloaded the
weapon with fingers trembling so badly that it was only
his sheer desperation that kept him from dumping his

spare shells off the side of the wagon completely.

Frank's head was facing forward, but his eyes were darting back and forth in a steady rhythm. Although most of his attention was focused on the team of horses, he was also watching the riders as they swept up to overtake the wagon.

As the other horses got closer, the pounding of their hooves could be felt even through the rattle and clamor of the wagon and its team. The gunshots were getting closer also. Every time there was a loud crack, there was a hiss like a hornet speeding past Frank and the younger man beside him.

The sound of Mikey closing his shotgun and snapping back the hammers was like music to both of their ears. The riders were getting close enough for their voices to be understood rather than just heard.

"Pull back on them reins," came a gruff command from one of the closest men on horseback.

Frank looked over and saw that the closest rider was still several yards away. With that in mind, he prayed that Mikey would do what he was supposed to and then he gave the reins a defiant snap. With that crack of leather, the team of horses let out a few startled whinnies and poured all of their strength into their strides.

With the animals' voices still sounding from in front of him, the next thing Frank heard was the roar of a shotgun blast coming from beside him. If he could spare the time or either of his hands, he swore he would have hugged the kid.

When he turned to look to his right, Frank was just in time to see that same rider fall from his saddle. So much blood was pouring from the rider's face that some of the fluid hung in the air like a crimson smudge on parchment even after his body had dropped. Without a rider in its saddle, the horse fell back and tore off in another direction.

The remaining riders, on the other hand, weren't so distracted. They didn't even seem to notice that one of their number had fallen, and they kept pressing to catch up with the speeding wagon. The only thing holding them back was that wayward horse, and once it was clear of the group, the rest were able to adjust themselves to the wagon's course.

"Last chance," came another voice from outside the wagon. "Pull this thing to a stop or we force you to."

Having killed his first man, Mikey felt his courage come flowing back into his bones. "Fuck you, assholes!" the young man shouted.

After that, Mikey must have gotten ready to empty his second barrel. That was the nearest that Frank could figure since he was forced to devote all of his attention to keeping the team in line. He knew the kid must have done something because the riders stopped giving ultimatums and went back to shooting.

This time, however, they all fired as one.

Unlike the last several volleys, not one of them missed.

Mikey was hit by so much lead that Frank could hear the gunfire punching through meat and bone as it damn near tore the younger man apart.

It should have been an easy job.

That's what he thought when the next bullet knocked him from the driver's seat.

THREE

The only thing worse than being unlucky was when a man had luck but didn't appreciate it. A man who didn't appreciate the good hands he'd been dealt never knew how to enjoy them, and he sure as hell didn't know how to make them work even more to his advantage. More than that, he didn't know how to simply savor the good in a world filled with so much bad.

Clint Adams didn't have either of those problems. He had his share of good luck and knew it. More importantly, he savored the good luck when it came since he knew that there would be plenty of times when good luck would be in short supply.

Then again, for a man in Clint's sort of life, it was hard not to know when the fickle eyes of fate were looking at him or away from him. More often than not, good luck meant he could live to see another day and bad luck meant spending a whole lot of time underground.

There was a good reason that gamblers referred to luck as a lady. She was a hard woman to court, but there were plenty of rewards at the end of the road. Of course, most of her favors only came to a man who worked damn hard to get them and when those pretty eyes were turned away altogether, the cold was almost unbearable.

Clint believed in making his own luck, but had also been around long enough to know that sometimes there just wasn't any use in trying to figure it out.

It was good luck when, just a week ago, he'd happened to spot a familiar name in the newspaper he'd been reading over dinner in Carson City. But it wasn't long before bad luck came into play once he read the entire story featuring the friend in question.

Frank Zeller was the kind of man who seemed like he could live forever. Clint had only met him on a handful of occasions, but the older man had left a big impression. Most of the work Frank did involved guarding something or someone from harm. It had been a job for the Union Pacific that had brought Clint and Frank together and the two had simply hit it off.

Kindred spirits.

Common interests.

Whatever it was that caused one person to take a shine to another didn't really matter. What did matter was that Clint considered Frank to be a good man and a good friend. Since neither of those things were easy to find, it didn't matter to Clint that he hadn't seen Frank Zeller in some time. What mattered was that Frank had come into some bad luck of his own and might not be too much longer for this hard world.

Bad luck, indeed.

Clint had been halfway through an excellent cut of prime rib with his coffee cooled to just the right temperature when he'd come across the story in his newspaper. By the time he'd finished reading it, his meal tasted sour in the back of his throat and his coffee had become bitter on his tongue.

He'd wound up reading the story through a few times

before finally putting the paper down and snagging the server who was walking past his table with an armload of dirty dishes.

"Excuse me," Clint said in a hasty voice. "I need to pay my bill and be on my way."

"All right, sir. I'll be right back."

Clint settled up his account not only with the restaurant, but with the hotel where he'd rented a room as well. From the time he stood up from his unfinished meal to the time he walked up to the front desk of the hotel with his saddlebags over his shoulder, Clint didn't say a word. His mind was swimming so deeply in the story he'd just read that he paid little attention his body went through its paces.

Stopping at the front desk, Clint was surprised to find that he still had the newspaper clutched in his hand.

"What's the matter, Mr. Adams?" the hotel clerk asked. "Read some bad news?"

Clint glanced at the paper in his hand and nodded. "Yeah. Real bad."

"What happened?"

"A friend of mine got hurt," Clint replied while handing over the money to settle his bill. "Got himself shot while riding on a job in Arizona. Near as I could tell, there wasn't even any reason for it."

The clerk took Clint's money and opened his cash drawer to fish out some change. "I think I read that story, too. Bunch of bandits shot up a wagon headed for Green Leaf, wasn't it?"

"Yeah. Actually, that was it."

"Terrible bit of news. You know the man that was killed?"

"No. I know the one that made it. At least, I hope he's still making it."

The clerk winced as though he'd already stepped on

Clint's toes. "My thoughts go out to your friend, Mr. Adams. Let's hope he pulls through better than that other boy he was riding with."

Clint had only found the story after flipping through several pages of articles and accounts of a more local nature. The story didn't even have any pictures, which made him even more surprised that the clerk would be so knowledgeable on the subject.

"I read the paper front to back," the clerk said as if knowing what Clint must have been thinking. "Even have some family in Arizona."

There was a dollar and some change on the counter, but Clint didn't pick it up. In fact, he even reached into his pocket to pull out a bit more money and set it down on top of the rest.

"Do you know if they have a telegraph office in Green Leaf?" Clint asked.

"I'm pretty sure they do."

"Then use some of that extra money to send a message to Frank Zeller or the closest relatives he might have there."

"What's the message?"

"Just tell him I'm coming."

FOUR

With an animal as fine as the Darley Arabian stallion that
had been given to Clint by P. T. Barnum himself, it was
a wonder how he could want anything faster. Still, no
matter how fast Eclipse ran, the stallion was no match for
what was racing toward Frank Zeller wherever he was
resting.

As far as Clint knew, the older man had already lost
his race with the Grim Reaper and was enjoying his final
rest. But Clint didn't want to think that way. He wanted
to think that even though news traveled slowly when ban-
ished to the tenth page of a paper, he could still make it
to Green Leaf in time to make a difference in a good
man's life.

He spurred Eclipse to cover the miles as fast as possible, but forced himself to ease up on the Darley Arabian
before causing damage to the well-meaning horse. It
seemed to Clint that Eclipse could feel his sense of ur-
gency and was doing his best to run faster even when
Clint was letting up on the reins.

It was several days of hard riding, but Clint found his
way into Arizona and within sight of the town called
Green Leaf. Now that he was close enough, he could see

why the place had been given that particular name. The town itself was surrounded on practically all sides by a wall of trees which still retained most of their healthy color even with the approach of winter.

Clint's mind had been so preoccupied with making the trip in as short a time as possible that he hadn't even been keeping track of the amount of days that had passed. It was less than a week, he knew, but not by much.

He knew Frank wouldn't be expecting him, which made Clint want to make the trip even more. The older man had been there for more than one sticky situation that could have gone very badly for Clint if he had been alone, and Clint didn't think it was right that Frank should be without his own backup.

Of course, as far as Clint knew, Frank could have an army of friends and relatives warming the boards at his bedside. But the two had had a few beers together, which was enough to make Clint fairly sure that Frank didn't have an army like that. From what Frank had said, he didn't even have any children who knew his name and the odds were that Frank's situation had remained the same.

The more Clint thought about that, the more he wanted to get to Green Leaf as quickly as possible. It wasn't until he actually had the town in his sight that a smile returned to Clint's face.

Eclipse was breathing heavily beneath him, but Clint urged the stallion to maintain his speed. "Come on, now," Clint said to the Darley Arabian. "We're almost there. I promise that I'll make this up to you with a nice, comfortable place to sleep and some greens to eat. How's that sound?"

Although the horse surely didn't understand Clint's words, he seemed to comprehend their meaning. Either that, or Eclipse was just too loyal to disappoint Clint by slowing down when he still had some strength left in his powerful body.

Clint rode through the tree line surrounding Green Leaf like a rock tossed through a plate glass window. Eclipse hadn't even come to a full stop before Clint swung down from the saddle and landed with both boots on the ground.

He got more than a few surprised glances by locals who'd been walking calmly about their business when he burst into their lives and looked wildly about. Tipping his hat to one of the more shocked ladies clutching a small child to her side, Clint caught his breath and headed for the closest, busiest street he could see.

It wasn't until he reached the stable that Clint realized just how worked up he was. Ever since he'd started the ride, he'd only had his troubled thoughts to keep him company. Well, he had those and Eclipse, but the horse wasn't much of a conversationalist. Now that he was in Green Leaf, Clint's mind settled enough for him to take a breath and settle himself just a bit.

He was just in time to keep from scaring off the lanky man who opened the stable door for him. Once Clint was inside the other man closed the door and said, "I can take them reins for you, mister. You look like you've had a hell of a ride."

"Thanks," Clint said, handing over the leather straps in his hand. "I'd appreciate it. I hope you've got a clean stall available."

"Sure do. I could even have my boy scrub your horse down and tuck him in at night."

"Perfect."

"That'll be an extra charge, of course," the stable man said with a bit of an apologetic tone.

"No problem." Clint gave Eclipse a pat on the shoulder and added, "He's earned it. Why don't you toss in a few greens for supper while you're at it."

The other man's face brightened and he led Eclipse to a large stall toward the front of the stable. When he turned around, he was just in time to snatch the silver dollar that Clint had flipped through the air toward him. "Will do! You need anything else, just let me—"

Before the offer could be completed, Clint was already taking him up on it. "Do you know where Frank Zeller is staying?"

The smile that had been on the stable man's face dimmed before fading away completely. "Oh . . . uhh . . . are you family?"

"No," Clint replied, his stomach twisting. "I'm a friend of his. Do you know where I can find him?"

"Turn right when you leave here. Head to the corner and make a left and keep walking. It'll be the fourth door on your right."

Clint tipped his hat. "Much obliged." As soon as he was outside, he started following the directions he'd been given. The only thing he could think about was how much he hoped he wasn't going to find himself at a funeral parlor.

FIVE

Clint's heart sank down to the bottom of his boots when he saw where he wound up at the end of the stable man's directions. The storefront was drab and dreary, but it was the ornate cross that truly told him he was in for some bad news.

Before he could get too saddened, however, he realized that he was looking at the wrong side of the street. When he turned around, he noticed a much more inviting door waiting for him. There was no sign, but at least it didn't look like an undertaker's place of business either. Clint walked up to the correct place and knocked a few times on the door.

He only had to wait a few moments before he heard the sound of someone coming to answer the door. It swung open to reveal a pretty young woman with short brown hair that fell in a soft curtain around her face.

"Yes?" the woman asked. "What can I do for you?"

Clint tried to look past her, but could only make out a chest of drawers and a wall beyond where she was standing. "Is Frank Zeller here?"

"Yes, he is. Are you family?"

"No, I'm a friend. My name's Clint Adams."

17

"Clint Adams?" came a gruff voice from farther back inside the building. "Let him in here, Layla."

Having recognized the voice, Clint was already smiling as the young woman stepped aside and allowed him to pass. There was a certain way that Frank had always talked which had stuck with Clint throughout the years. He'd remembered it especially as of late because he'd been hoping to hear that voice from the moment he'd started his ride to town.

Clint hurried inside and found himself in a small room filled mostly with cabinets, a coat rack and a rolltop desk. Beyond that was another room which was much larger. In fact, it seemed about double the size of a modest house and was filled with two rows of narrow beds and a large table in the center of the room covered with pitchers of water and clean, neatly folded towels.

Most of the dozen or so beds were empty. Of the ones that were occupied, two of them had elderly women sleeping in them, one had a small child with a yellow taint to his skin and the other contained the very man that Clint had been hoping to find.

"Hello there, Frank," Clint said as he strode over to the older man's bedside. "It sure is good to see you."

"Well, I didn't even know you were lookin' for me. Damn, it's been a long time, Clint. What the hell have you been up to?"

"I've been up to plenty, Frank, but at least I haven't gotten myself shot too badly. And here I thought you were smart enough to stay out of the way once the lead started flying."

Frank rolled his eyes and started to scoot up in his bed so he could sit upright. The effort caused him to suck in a sharp breath as his face twisted into a painful expression.

Reaching out, Clint wasn't sure what to do, so he paused before touching so much as Frank's shoulder. "Should you be sitting up?" he asked.

When he saw that Frank wasn't about to answer right away, Clint looked toward the young brown-haired woman who was still nearby. He was just in time to step out of the way before she pushed him aside on her way to Frank's bed.

"You know you're not supposed to get out of bed yet, Mr. Zeller," the young woman said. Despite her soft voice, she took hold of him like she had the ability to toss him out a window. Even with her strong movements, she handled him with just enough force to push him back under the covers and not cause him any more pain.

"Goddammit," Frank grumbled. "I just want to sit up so I can talk to my friend here. Is that so wrong?"

"Of course not, but I've told you plenty of times that if you don't sit still, these wounds are never going to heal." The young woman fretted with Frank's pillow and blankets, easing up considerably once she had him tucked away right where she wanted him. By the tone in her voice, it seemed that she was more than used to the old man's grousing.

As for Frank, he continued to squirm, but wasn't actively trying to get out from under the blankets. Instead, his fidgeting seemed more like general shifting rather than trying to get out of bed. Between him and the woman who was obviously his nurse, he got himself up enough to rest his shoulders against the headboard.

"Is this all right?" Frank asked the nurse sarcastically. "Can I talk now without you fussing over me like I'm some kind of baby in a bassinet?"

Rather than answer his question, she turned to Clint and gave him an apologetic smile. "Sorry about that, but if I don't step in every now and then, Frank would just try to walk out of here."

Clint returned her smile and said, "Forget about it. I came here to make sure he was all right and it looks like you're doing your job pretty well. Is this a hospital? I didn't see any sign outside."

"It's a place for Doctor Grant's patients to recover where they can be looked after and seen to." She leaned in a little closer to Clint and lowered her voice to a whisper. "You can sit and visit for a while, but not for too long. I'd also appreciate it if you could talk him into taking his medicine. I haven't had much luck in that area."

With Layla standing so close, Clint could smell the clean, powdery scent of her skin. Although there wasn't any perfume on her, she had the scent of a beautiful woman, which was distinctive and different to each one. A few wisps of her hair brushed over his cheek, sending a chill through Clint's skin.

"I can't make any guarantees," Clint said. "But I'll try."

She smiled at him warmly. "Thank you, Mr. Adams."

"Please. Call me Clint."

Layla nodded once and stepped past him so she could tend to the child in the bed nearby. She moved so lightly that Clint found it hard to believe that she could manhandle Frank the way she'd just done. When he looked back toward the old man, Clint found him grinning back at him and shaking his head.

"Same ol' Clint," Frank said. "Any female in your line of sight and you start circling."

"Last time we ran into each other, I was the one showing up in the newspapers. That much sure has changed."

"Newspapers? What are you talking about?"

"I think you know what I'm talking about," Clint said, pulling up a chair and sitting down next to Frank's bed. "If we were in a saloon somewhere, you might have a better chance at pretending you're in perfect health. Trying to pull that bluff from a hospital bed won't quite cut it."

"Yeah, I guess even you'd be too sharp to miss that one, huh?"

"The story I read said there was a robbery." Just saying that brought back much of the concern that had led Clint all the way to Green Leaf. "What happened? How bad are you hurt?"

Frank shook his head, his hand drifting toward the bandages wrapped around his torso. "It was the damnedest thing, Clint. I've had a few weeks to think about it and I still don't know why we got robbed."

"Come on, now. You'd been guarding shipments for years back when we worked that job together. These things happen."

"Sure they do. They happen when the cargo is worth somethin'. They happen when there's half a reason for it." Frank shifted and looked straight into Clint's eyes. "We were hauling lumber, Clint. It was on a flatbed wagon, so there was no way for anyone with eyes in their head to miss it. There wasn't even a strongbox."

Clint tried to be comforting as he sat and listened. He even tried to keep from looking worried about what he was hearing. Unfortunately, that was becoming more difficult with every passing second.

SIX

"Maybe it was a mistake," Clint offered.

Frank shook his head. "No mistake. I saw their eyes and the way they rode and even the way they shot. They were doin' just what they wanted to do. Near as I can figure, there was only one thing that happened that they didn't plan."

"What's that?"

"I lived."

Even when he'd read that newspaper story over and over again, Clint hadn't thought it was anything more than a robbery. There wasn't much in the story apart from the event itself and the names of the men that were hurt. He figured that as long as Frank was alive and recovering, things were on their way to getting better.

Now, Clint wasn't so sure. He did know one thing for sure: things were a hell of a long way from getting better. In fact, they were going in the exact opposite direction.

"So what are you telling me?" Clint asked, moving forward until he was literally sitting on the edge of his seat. "Do you think those men were out to kill you and your partner? Is there someone out there who wants to see you dead that badly?"

Frank shook his head and let out a big breath in frustration. "No, that's not what I think. I've pissed off plenty of people in my time, but not anyone who'd go through that much trouble to kill me. Hell, all they need to do is look for me in a saloon whenever I ain't working.

"I think that they wanted to kill anyone who was riding on that wagon with that shipment. That's what I've come up with. I've been thinking it over the whole time I've been resting up here. Believe me, a man gets an awfully clear head when all he has to think about is staying alive. Once it stopped hurting to breathe, I could only focus on one thing—what happened the day when Mikey was killed."

For a moment, Clint recognized that other name but wasn't able to put his finger on where he'd heard it. He was soon nodding and saying, "That was the man riding shotgun with you that day."

"Man?" Frank scoffed without any humor in his voice. "He was barely old enough to get whiskers on his chin. He held that gun of his like he was out hunting with his pappy." Suddenly, Frank clenched his fists and pounded at the side of his bed. The impact echoed throughout the room, drawing the attention of every open eye in the place.

"I should'a known better," Frank snarled. He didn't seem to notice anyone else looking at him. He didn't even seem to notice Clint sitting right there beside him. "I've been riding across this country for most'a my life. I should'a known that kid wasn't ready to pull no trigger.

"I saw those men coming before he did. I was the one who knew what to do. They started firing before either of us expected it. There was so much lead in the air, I should've just turned the wagon around. I should've done something different. Anything! Mikey's blood might just as well be on my own han—"

"That's enough, Frank," Clint interrupted sharply.

When he saw that he hadn't gotten through to the older man just yet, Clint stood up and lowered himself so one hand was resting on either side of the bed frame. "Stop it right there."

Behind Clint, Layla was on her way over. She stopped and waited before moving him aside, watching to see what Clint would do next.

The expression on Clint's face might have been mistaken for anger due to its intensity. When he spoke, however, there was no anger in his voice. There was just stern determination.

"If you knew what was going to happen, would you do anything differently?" Clint asked.

"Of course I would."

"And did you know what was going to happen?"

"Clint, just sit bac—"

"Answer the question!"

Frank glared at Clint and spoke without moving anything but his lips. "No. I didn't know."

"Then none of this is your fault. Jesus Christ, you almost got killed in that robbery. From what it said in that story, you even managed to take out one of the robbers before it was all over."

"Nah. That was the kid's doing. All I did was drive."

Clint moved back from Frank and took a look at the other man's injuries. Besides the bandages around his torso, Frank's face was bruised and there were several nasty cuts on the sides of his head. One in particular caught his attention because it was twice the size of the rest and had been stitched up with black thread.

"How many bullets did you take?" Clint asked.

"One in the knee and another in the shoulder." He flexed his left arm, but gave up as pain wracked his entire body. "The fall from the wagon hurt more'n the bullets though."

Clint lowered himself into his chair. He could hear

Layla behind him reassuring one of the other patients. She must have thought Clint was doing a good enough job on his own because she walked away to let him deal with Frank without her stepping in.

"You said you got a look at the robbers," Clint pointed out. "You can remember them pretty well?"

"Remember 'em pretty well?" Frank asked. "After what they done to me and Mikey, I won't ever forget them."

"And you say you're pretty sure they knew what they were doing."

Frank started to laugh, but the effort must have sent a jolt of pain through him because he quickly stopped with a wince. "I've been riding shotgun or driving for plenty of years and have been at gunpoint plenty of times. I know good robbers from bad ones. These boys had everything together. That is, except for one thing."

"What's that?"

"Masks. They weren't wearing any."

"So you got a look at them?"

"One of 'em. The one that put me and Mikey down. It was Sonny Byrnes. You heard of him?"

Clint nodded. "Oh yeah. I sure have. I know enough about him to be sure that you being alive today is either the biggest stroke of luck on record or something that was meant to happen from the start."

"So which do you think it is?"

"No offense, Frank, but nobody's that lucky."

SEVEN

There were two kinds of reputations a man could have. There were the ones that were started by words and those started by action. Being the owner of a reputation himself, Clint knew about them pretty well. He didn't learn it by choice, like the men that wanted to be known for whatever reason. He learned it by being saddled with a reputation and not being able to ride fast enough to outrun it.

His was a reputation started by his own actions. Good or bad, what Clint did was told to others and word spread until his name became widely known. Because of that reputation, he came across plenty of others looking to make one for themselves.

The ones looking to build a reputation on words were nothing more than blowhards and usually couldn't fool much of anyone. He found before too long that the ones to watch out for were those looking to make their reputation through their own actions.

They were the ones who would seek out a fight and were oftentimes too stupid to know they couldn't win it. And within that group, there were a few truly dangerous men. They were dangerous because they weren't out for a reputation at all. They'd simply killed too many or stolen too much to go unnoticed any longer.

Sonny Byrnes was one of those men.

Clint hadn't met the infamous killer and thief personally, but he'd been asked to hunt down the outlaw on more than one occasion. He'd even accepted a few of those offers because the crimes committed had been the ones that Clint couldn't just let pass.

Sonny Byrnes was wanted for countless murders with victims ranging from would-be gunslingers to sleeping wives whose only crime was to spurn the attention of a husband with enough money to hire a killer. His robberies were quick and coldhearted. His style was to kill everyone in the area and then take their money. That went for banks, stores, stagecoaches, even a church or two when times got hard.

Sonny Byrnes was one of those men that seemed to disappear. Some of the best trackers in the country had gone after him, including Clint Adams himself. What they found was always the same: nothing.

Well, that wasn't entirely true. Clint had come across a few more bodies. They were the bodies of the only folks who might have known where to find Sonny Byrnes. Most of those bodies had been young women who'd shared Sonny's bed and had become a liability in the process.

All of that flooded through Clint's mind in the pause between the last time anyone had spoken. In that time, Frank had had enough of a chance to notice the change that had come over Clint's face.

"You alright, Clint?" he asked.

Clint's brow furrowed a bit as he snapped his attention back onto the wounded man in front of him. "Yeah. Just thinking, that's all."

Frank shifted in his bed and nodded solemnly. "I take it by the look on your face that you know Sonny Byrnes plenty well. Any decent man who knows what that animal did would look just as haunted as you do."

"You're sure it was him?" Clint asked. "I mean, Sonny isn't the kind of man to leave someone alive when he pulls a job."

"And he's also not the type of man to bother with robbing a wagon full of timber and nails. He's not the kind to charge in at the wrong target either."

"It could have been an honest mistake. Well, so to speak."

"Come on now, Clint. I may have gotten hurt, but I didn't take a knock on the head. First-timers make mistakes like that. Assholes with nothing but sod between their ears make mistakes like that. Sonny Byrnes is a professional. If he came up on the wrong wagon, he would have steered away before it got too serious. He's done it before."

"I know."

Frank cocked his head and looked genuinely surprised. "You do? How?"

"Because that's how I almost caught him."

"I never heard about that one."

"Because we haven't seen each other for a while and unlike some people, my every move doesn't wind up in the newspaper."

"You'd be hard-pressed to convince me of that, but your point's taken."

Clint leaned back and glanced over to where the nurse was standing. Layla gave him a nod to let him know that it was fine for him to stay just a little bit longer.

"I worked on a posse a few years back," Clint said. "It was down in New Mexico for a sheriff named Terranova who was going after Sonny Byrnes. I set up a ripe target to bait Sonny into an ambush that would lead the entire gang into a jail cell."

"Really? What happened?"

"Sonny rode right up to it and knew it wasn't what he was after. He sniffed it out in seconds and turned back. We gave him a hell of a chase, but in the end he just knew the land better than anyone else and got away. He may have lost his edge in the meantime, but I doubt it."

Frank laughed at that. "The good ones like Sonny don't lose their edge. They just keep getting sharper."

"It sounds like you know this man better than I do," Clint observed.

"It's my business to know who might be after the shipments I'm guarding. He took more than one out from under me throughout the years. I'm not proud of it, but with someone as sharp as Sonny Byrnes, it's not something to be ashamed of either."

After hearing what Frank had to say and mixing it in with his own memories of the man in question, Clint wound up shaking his head. He could feel the tiredness creeping into his eyes and when he rubbed them, it only seemed to make the fatigue sink in that much deeper.

Layla's footsteps were coming up behind him, followed by the soft touch of her hand upon his shoulder. "Frank needs his rest, Mr. Adams," she said.

"Yeah," Frank said to him. "You look like you need yours as well."

Standing up, Clint smiled at both the wounded man and his nurse. "Suddenly, I get the feeling that I'm not wanted."

Layla lowered her eyes and blushed a bit around the cheeks. Those two little things were enough to tell Clint that he couldn't have been farther from the truth.

"It's just for now," she said after quickly regaining her composure. "You're welcome to visit again tomorrow."

Frank grumbled a bit, but waved Clint off as though the end of visiting hours was his own idea. He shot Clint a glance that showed a wariness that went much farther than just the damage that had been done to his body.

There was something else troubling him that had only been brought closer to the surface by his most recent conversation.

Clint knew that because he was feeling that same uneasiness himself.

"Come back anytime, Mr. Adams," Layla said, interrupting Clint's thoughts. "I'm usually here, so you don't have to worry about scheduled visiting hours."

"That's good," Clint replied. "Because I don't have a clue what that schedule might be."

She smiled a little too much at that small joke, but Clint wasn't about to complain. Her face was smooth and beautiful. When she walked him to the front door, she held his hand lightly as though she didn't even know that she was doing it.

"Perhaps I could even see you outside of visiting hours," she said. "Outside of here, even."

Although Clint thought he would have to make the first move in that direction, he wasn't about to complain. "That sounds great. How about tomorrow?"

She nodded and smiled once again. Perhaps Frank's luck was holding up after all. Clint could sure think of plenty worse things than having someone like Layla tucking him in every night.

EIGHT

Green Leaf, Arizona, was a nice town, but so far Clint felt as though he'd barely seen any of it. When he'd arrived, he'd been so focused on seeing Frank that he was hardly paying attention to anything else. Now that he stepped out with his mind somewhat at ease, it was too dark to see more than the shapes of buildings and the occasional backlit window.

A dog was barking in the distance. It wasn't the deep voice of a hound or hunting dog, but one of those little yappers that would have been more at home on a rich woman's lap. Apart from that, Clint could hear the sound of voices coming from one direction, so that was the direction he chose when he started walking.

Before long, he could see the saloon that was the source of the voices. Either there or someplace nearby, he figured he could find a hotel. He might have already gotten directions to a hotel from any number of people, but the advice would have fallen upon deaf ears. Clint was still distracted, but in a different way from when he'd arrived. Now, he was more concerned with the story he'd heard from Frank Zeller about the robbery that had put his friend in that sick bed.

31

It was a concern that sharpened his senses. Clint felt
as though he was aware of every movement around him
as well as every set of eyes turned his way. As uncomfortable as it might have been, those were the instincts
that kept him alive.

There was a hotel in sight, but Clint stopped to lean
against the post of a nearby awning so he could take a
few breaths. The fresh air did him a lot of good. The stars
were coming out and looking up toward them helped to
divert his attention.

Unfortunately, the diversion didn't do its job for very
long.

As much as he didn't want to look a gift horse in the
mouth, Clint knew that Frank's being alive wasn't just a
happy coincidence. If Frank was alive, that meant Sonny
Byrnes hadn't killed him. And if Sonny hadn't killed him,
it had been on purpose.

That would explain why there had been so much shooting at the start of the robbery without anyone getting hit.
But that didn't explain why none of the robbers had been
wearing masks. Under those circumstances, Clint figured
that any professional criminal would have made doubly
sure that there were no witnesses drawing breath.

Frank hadn't just survived the robbery. He'd been allowed to live. With that being the case, there was only
one conclusion to draw.

Sonny Byrnes had wanted there to be one survivor and
one survivor only. In that respect, perhaps Frank had been
damn lucky. Clint was sure that the kid riding shotgun on
that wagon would certainly agree with that.

Clint was feeling tired. It seemed as though the entire
day as well as a few before it were all bearing down on
him at once. His bones started to ache and his eyelids
were getting heavier by the second. Using his last bit of
steam to keep his legs moving, Clint headed to the hotel
he'd spotted and got a room. By the time he walked

through the door and saw the bed he'd rented, he felt like he couldn't even hold his saddlebags anymore.

The bags hit the floor hard and Clint dropped onto the bed even harder. After rolling onto his back and kicking off his boots, he folded his hands across his belly and stretched out on the mattress. He was asleep about two seconds later.

It was the kind of sleep that felt like a reward to a tired body. There were no dreams and no restless shifting. There was only the quiet blackness behind Clint's eyelids and the sensation of being suspended in nothingness.

More importantly, it was the kind of sleep that anyone would hate to give up. Clint was no exception to that and was put into a foul mood the instant he was pulled out of his slumber by a rapping on his door. The noise wasn't much, but it didn't take much to yank him out of the sleep that had come upon him so quickly. In fact, he didn't even realize he'd left his gun belt on until his hand reflexively slapped against his modified Colt.

"Who's there?" Clint snarled as he swung his feet over the side of the bed and forced his eyes to focus.

At first, there was no response. The knocking had stopped, but Clint could see by the shadow coming from under his door that whoever had waken him was still standing there.

Clint pulled in a deep breath and walked to the door. Standing to one side just in case the visitor wasn't the friendly sort, he kept his hand over his gun and spoke again in a less abrasive tone. "Who is it?"

"It's me, Clint," came a soft, familiar voice. "Layla."

"Layla? But it's . . ." He paused to take a look at his watch, but since he hadn't turned his lantern on he couldn't see it. "It's late."

"I know. I could come back some other time."

Hearing the disappointment in her voice, Clint flipped

the latch on the door and opened it. He forced a friendly smile onto his face so he wouldn't scare her off the moment she saw him. That smile became genuine when he got a look at what was waiting for him on the other side of that door.

Layla was still dressed in the simple dress that she'd been in when Clint had visited Frank. This time, however, she looked much more disheveled. Her short brown hair was unruly and stray wisps hung in her face. Her clothes were rumpled after a hard day's work and the top two buttons of her dress had been pulled apart to reveal the upper slope of her small, pert breasts.

"I know it's late," she said. "But I was hoping you'd still be up."

There was a soft sensuality in her voice and the way she looked up at him while keeping her head tilted slightly down made her look even more attractive. Her lips were thin and a shade of pink that made him certain they were every bit as soft as they looked.

Stepping aside, he said, "Well, I was sleeping but I'm up now. Come on in."

NINE

All of the sternness that had been in Layla's posture when looking over her patients was gone. That forcefulness of her personality now melted into something much more feminine and undeniably erotic as she confidently strode into Clint's room as if it belonged to her.

"What brings you here, Layla?" Clint asked, although he was getting plenty of ideas of his own.

She stopped just short of the bed, turned around and faced him with a warm, comforting smile. "Just a feeling I got when we were talking before. I felt like if things were different, or if we were somewhere else, you wouldn't have left so soon." The familiar flush returned to her cheeks and she took her eyes away from him for a moment. "I could be wrong, but I hope I'm not."

Clint stepped up to her and put his finger beneath her chin. From there, he lifted her face so he could look straight at her as he said, "You're far from wrong. When we were talking before, I was actually thinking how lucky Frank was that he got to have you so close for so long."

She didn't shy away from his touch. On the contrary, she stepped forward until her body brushed against his. Clint could feel her heat against his skin even though there

were layers of clothing separating them. Both of them
were trying to restrain themselves but were having a difficult time doing so. That much was apparent by the tenseness that could be felt in both of their muscles.

"I've learned a lot in my job," she said. "The main
thing is that life is a fragile thing and it doesn't take much
for it to come to an end. I've seen too many people leave
this world with regrets."

"And you don't want to be one of them?"

She shook her head, but that smile quickly burned
brighter again as she added, "But that all might just be
some fancy talk for me to justify coming up here to you
like this."

Clint shrugged and moved forward so his lips brushed
against hers as he said, "Either one works just fine for
me."

When they kissed, it felt as if Clint's entire body was
letting out a breath that had been held for too long. Seeing
her at his door had stirred something inside of him that
had only grown until it felt like it would burst inside of
him. Now that he was giving in to his desires, he felt that
tenseness fading away.

It was obvious that she was feeling the same thing.
Possibly it was even more powerful than what had come
over Clint. Layla's body melted into Clint's arms and her
lips parted after only a few seconds of their kiss. She was
the one to start nibbling his lips as though he was the
meal that she'd been craving for so long. Her little tongue
extended to lick him, sending flashes of heat throughout
Clint's entire body.

As he moved his hands over her body, Clint got the
fleeting thought that he might be having a dream. Her hips
pressed against him in just the right way and she moaned
a little every time he touched her in a new place. When
the palm of his hand slid over her breast, Clint could feel
her erect nipples through the fabric of her dress.

He could also feel her hands busily exploring his own body. First she felt the contour of his chest and then quickly slid down to the hardening column of flesh between his legs.

"Oh, God, I've wanted this," she whispered as she leaned back to savor the feel of his hands upon her. "Just please don't stop."

That was all Clint needed to hear as he reached down to cup her buttocks in his hands and lift her up off the floor. She followed his lead immediately and hopped up into his arms so he could carry her across the floor and onto the bed.

They both fell down onto the mattress in a heap of writhing bodies. The noise of the bed groaning beneath them made them pause for a moment as if neither one of them could believe what they were doing. Layla looked at the door as if she expected it to open at any moment. When she looked back, Clint was glancing around in much the same way.

"You look like you want to get out of here," Clint said jokingly.

She gave him another smile, paused and then tossed her head back against the mattress. "I was just wondering if we were making enough noise to wake the whole hotel."

"I'm not sure, but that gives me something to shoot for."

They laughed together and slowly their hands picked up right where they'd left off. It wasn't long before they passed the point where they'd left off before and quickly moved on to feeling beneath the other's clothing, their fingers touching warm, naked flesh.

Clint fumbled a bit with her dress, mainly because he didn't want to rip it off of her. Well, he may have wanted to, but didn't think she would be too crazy about that idea. He found her to be very accommodating, however, and

lifted or shifted just perfectly to allow him to peel the
dress away from her body and finally over her head.

Layla, on the other hand, had no trouble whatsoever
separating Clint from his clothes. In fact, she was done
so quickly that Clint was lying there stripped completely
naked and looking at her with no small amount of surprise.

"Practice makes perfect," she said with a shrug. "I
could've undressed you if you were dead asleep. And
don't think that I wasn't considering that when you took
so long to open that door earlier."

"Oh really? Should I guess what else you were thinking about?"

Layla shifted on the bed and pulled Clint down on top
of her. Spreading her legs open, she wrapped them around
his waist and moved her hips so she could ease her wet
vagina against the length of Clint's cock.

"It went something like this," she said, savoring the
mixture of surprise and pleasure written all over Clint's
face. The more she moved, the wetter she became until
finally her head dropped back against the mattress as she
let out a purring breath.

Clint was getting so hard that he knew he would ache
if he didn't get inside of her soon. All it took was a few
more shifts and one forward push for him to feel the tip
of his penis slide between the lips of her pussy and into
her warm depths.

Layla's legs tightened around him and the purring
sound she was making turned into a full throated groan.
She no longer seemed to care about waking anyone else
around her and she let out an even louder moan when
he'd driven his cock all the way inside of her.

Propping himself up using one hand, Clint started to
move in and out of her in a gentle rhythm. She was so
wet by now that his cock glided between her legs as he
entered her again and again. He let his free hand wander

over her body, gently massaging her firm little breasts, every so often rubbing her nipple between his thumb and forefinger. That sent a shiver through Layla's body that even Clint could feel. Whenever she tensed, the lips between her thighs would tense around him as well.

Finally, she allowed herself to open her eyes and watch him as he rocked forward and back on top of her. Layla's eyes would widen whenever he penetrated her fully and she would let out a slow breath as he pulled his rigid penis almost completely out of her.

She could only tolerate that sensual teasing so much. Then she couldn't take it any more. Allowing her legs to loosen from where they'd been locked around his waist, she put her feet against the bed and opened her thighs even wider. From there, she started pumping her own hips in time to Clint's thrusts.

"Do it harder," she urged in a nasty whisper. "Harder like this."

Saying that, she pumped her hips quicker, making Clint want to do just as she'd asked so he could keep up. But he only did as she'd requested for so long, then he took the reins back into his own hands.

Clint sat up so his back was straight and he was kneeling between her legs. Using both hands to take hold of her hips and tight little backside, he lifted her off the bed and pulled her toward him as he pumped forward with his hips.

That took Layla by surprise and she let out a scream that echoed throughout the room and didn't stop until there was hardly any breath left in her body. She reached both hands over her head and took hold of the sheets near the pillow while arching her back and sliding one leg around Clint's waist. With that one leg, she could pull him closer when she wanted him to go faster or just hang on when his pace was just right.

With that rhythm established, Clint and Layla moved

as one person. All one of them had to do was think about what they wanted and soon the other one was giving it to them. The instant Clint thought he was reaching the end of his strength, Layla would pump harder, working his cock in and out of her.

And when she could no longer maintain that effort, Clint was there to pick her up again and take control. Her body seemed to melt around him and the few times when he slipped out of her, he could see the disappointment on Layla's face. That expression only lasted until his rigid penis was once again sliding between the wetness of her lips and the whole ride started all over again.

They climaxed together. Each of them let out a satisfied groan that could be felt all the way down to their toes. By the time Clint could pull in another breath, he and Layla were collapsing on top of each other and sleep overtook them both.

TEN

Clint woke up the next morning with a start. He snapped awake as though someone had doused him with cold water and when he looked beside him he saw that he was alone in the bed. He could still feel the warmth of Layla's body beside him and could practically taste her as if it had only been moments ago that his lips had been pressed against hers.

As he took a few deep breaths to clear his head, he swung his feet over the side of the bed and started working out the kinks in his neck. He figured there was no reason for her to have spent the entire night in his room. In fact, having her gone when he awoke made the previous night seem even more like a dream.

That was when it struck him.

Not only was he alone in bed, but he was fully dressed. His hat had fallen off his chest when he sat up and his gun belt was still strapped around his waist. Clint froze where he was sitting and thought back to the previous night's encounter.

Layla's voice still echoed in his head, but only in his mind. The more he thought about touching her and feeling her naked skin, the more Clint was convinced that it had

41

indeed been a dream. It was a vivid and very, very good dream, but a dream nonetheless.

The only proof he needed of that besides his own opinion was his gun belt. It was odd enough for him to fall asleep on a good bed wearing his Colt, but he sure as hell wouldn't have dressed and buckled it back on if he'd spent the night with Layla right beside him.

Clint laughed to himself and shed the clothes that he'd been wearing since the day before. In moments, he was dressed and had splashed his face with some water from the basin on the table by the bed. The cool liquid felt great against his skin, energizing him just as much as the solid sleep he'd gotten.

Well, on second thought, the water felt good, but not as good as the dream that had filled the previous night's rest.

Hoping all the sounds he'd made last night had only been in his dream as well, Clint left his room and headed for the lobby of the hotel. He didn't get any strange looks, so he figured that he'd kept to himself the night before.

"Mornin'," the clerk at the front desk said in a chipper tone. "Hope you slept alright."

"I slept good," Clint replied. "Really good. You know where I can get some breakfast?"

"The place across the street is as good as any. They should still be serving breakfast for a while yet."

Clint checked his pocket watch and saw it was only creeping up on eight o'clock in the morning. When he stepped outside, he got a full taste of the crisp morning air which was even more like a bucket full of cold water tossed in his face.

The autumn sky was only starting to brighten and the breeze still had the bite of cold on its tongue. Having spent plenty of time the other day thinking about luck, Clint couldn't help but feel pretty damn lucky to be alive on a morning like this one. No matter what else was going on in his life, Clint never lost sight of the simple pleasures like waking up on a crisp, autumn morning or eating a good meal.

Clint always savored every meal, taking the time to enjoy each bite as it came. The place across the street from the hotel was a long building that reminded Clint of a meal hall on a large ranch. Although the place wasn't much more than twenty feet or so across, the long tables with benches on either side made it seem bigger.

Clint ordered a plate of eggs, potatoes, biscuits and gravy. The server who brought the food couldn't have been more than twenty-two or so and was a little too skinny for Clint. But the more food she brought out, the better it tasted and the prettier that little waitress became.

Finishing off the last of the meal was enough to put a satisfied grin on Clint's face. He settled up the bill and stepped outside to see the sun making its first real appearance of the day. With the warmth of the daylight on his skin, Clint pulled in another breath of fresh air and bought a newspaper before starting to walk toward the more familiar part of town.

Even as he started thinking about what he had discussed with Frank earlier, Clint was unable to feel too hopeless. In fact, the perfect night's sleep combined with the fresh air and hearty meal had done him wonders. But it wasn't until his eyes roamed over a story in the newspaper that he came up with the very thing he needed.

A plan.

ELEVEN

"Good morning, Mr. Adams," came the sweet voice that had become all too familiar in Clint's mind.

Layla was still dressed simply, but this time she was wearing a white cotton dress with pink stripes running down her sides. She looked freshly scrubbed and wide-eyed as she waved to him, walking toward the front door as Clint stepped into the infirmary.

Even though he knew his most recent encounter with Layla had been a dream, Clint couldn't help but feel a little awkward in her presence. The dream had been so vivid and was so fresh in his mind that Clint felt as though he'd been given an inside glimpse into the woman's most private of moments.

Smiling at him, Layla pointed out, "Why Clint, you're blushing."

He rolled his eyes and cleared his throat, prompting her to back up a step and rush to correct herself.

"It's all right that I call you Clint, isn't it?"

"Sure it is," he said, wanting to say a little more to put her at ease. Instead, he just settled for, "Mind if I have a word with Frank?"

"He's an early riser. Go on ahead."

Clint returned the woman's friendly smile and couldn't keep his eyes from wandering over the curves of her body. His memory was even better than he thought because as near as he could tell, his imagination had been pretty close to her real dimensions. The little flush that came to her cheeks seemed especially sexy with that in mind.

"She's a beaut, ain't she?" Frank said as Clint walked up to his bedside.

"Pardon me?"

"No need to act any different around me. I'm a man just the same as you. Hell, it's goddamn torture to have a filly like that tuck me in at night when I'm still laid up in here."

Clint pulled up a chair and sat down next to Frank, pretending to not be so intimately familiar with what the older man was talking about. "Is that all you've been thinking about with all this free time?"

"Heh. I suppose you could think of something better?"

"I sure can. How about a way to make sure that what happened to you won't happen to anyone else again? And while I'm at it, how about if I find out just why the hell your shipment was attacked in the first place?"

Frank's eyes narrowed. "You got my attention."

"I've been thinking about everything you told me. After that, I put together everything I read in that newspaper story and I came up with a couple different accounts. First of all, the newspaper account sounded pretty straightforward, like a plain robbery that went very bad.

"What you told me, on the other hand, sounds anything but simple. There were too many things that didn't fit. Hell," Clint said, "there were plenty of things that just plain didn't make sense."

Frank let out an exasperated breath and shook his head. "I may have remembered it wrong, with all the shooting and all. Still, I don't think my memory's that bad."

"I'm not doubting your memory," Clint said reassur-

ingly. "I know you well enough to trust what you say.
You've been doing this job for too long to mix up things
like what you told me."

"So where does that leave us?"

"It left me with a real bad feeling in my gut. That is,
up until things started to fit together in my head. Sonny
Byrnes is a known man. More than that, he's a known
robber. Known killers are usually wild and bloodthirsty.
Robbers aren't exactly angels, but they're smarter than
mad dog killers. They've got to be, otherwise they would
be prisoners and not out making names for themselves."

"True enough."

"Sonny wanted you to live. He also wanted you to see
his face so you could spread the word about what had
happened."

"I came up with that on my own, but it all falls apart
at the same place. Why would he do that?"

Clint wanted to step in with an explanation, but it simply wasn't there. Instead, he just started to feel the same
exasperation that was plain enough to see on Frank's face.
"I don't know that yet, but it's got to be more than just
to add credits to his name. Sonny's too far along to be
worried about that. He's a good enough robber to know
it's so much better to work as a ghost than a known man."

"So that leaves us right where we started."

"Not exactly. If Sonny wasn't out to make a name for
himself and he wasn't out to kill both of you—"

"I can't say for sure that he wasn't out to kill us both.
I barely escaped with my life."

Clint took another look at Frank and shook his head.
"You said there was a lot of shooting to herd you in the
proper direction, right?"

"Yeah."

"And with all that shooting, neither you or your partner
were hit until one of their own men was killed. Am I still
right?"

Frank nodded.

"They didn't even hit the horses, which takes more control than to put a round through a team of big animals. I'll bet when they did shoot your partner, that kid was dead before he hit the ground."

A haunted look came across Frank's eyes and some of the color drained from his skin. Finally, he nodded one last time.

"You were just as close to Sonny as your partner was," Clint said in a calm, level voice. "You took one hit, fell, and nobody even checked to see if you were moving?"

"Sonny checked."

"But he didn't finish you off, even though he's known for leaving nothing but bodies and empty bank vaults wherever he goes." After letting that sink in, Clint added, "He let you live for some damn good reason. All we need to do is find out what that reason was."

"How do you propose to do that?"

"I'll get it straight from Sonny's own mouth."

Frank's head snapped back as though he'd been struck.

TWELVE

Not only did Frank look like he'd been gut-kicked by a mule, but he also seemed to have lost his voice as well. For a few minutes after Clint told him what he had up his sleeve, Frank tried to talk but simply couldn't find the words. His mouth opened and closed. A few breaths came out, but not one sound could be heard.

In fact, the older man looked so odd that he attracted the attention of the woman in charge of keeping him as normal as possible. Layla walked quickly over to his bed-side and bent over so she could put her ear close to Frank's mouth.

"Are you all right?" she asked Frank as well as Clint.

Unable to keep his eyes off of her trim little backside, Clint said, "He's fine. Just a little winded."

That got Frank's words flowing again. "Winded?" he said. "Damn shocked is more like it!"

Layla pulled her ear away just in time to keep herself from being deafened by Frank's sudden outburst. Shaking her head, she felt his forehead and patted him down with a damp cloth. "You shouldn't scare me like that," she scolded.

"But you're so precious when you're riled up like

that," the older man said, giving Clint a quick, knowing wink.

She straightened up and left the cloth on Frank's head. "Yep. I'd say you're just fine." When she turned to Clint, she gave him a smile as well as a bashful turn of her eyes.

It seemed to him as though she either knew exactly what he was thinking or had been having some pretty sweet dreams of her own. Whichever it was, Clint didn't mind so long as she kept those smiles coming.

"I'll let you two get back to your conversation," she said after shaking off whatever was bringing the flush to her cheeks. "And don't cry wolf again, Frank."

"Yes, ma'am," he said with a salute. Once his nurse had gone back to another bedside, Frank looked back to Clint and said, "You must be out of your damn mind. Or you're kidding me. Is that it?"

"Nope. I'm dead serious." Clint stopped himself and added, "Well, that was a bad choice of words, but you know what I mean."

"I know what you mean and if you're serious, then I don't think that was a bad choice of words at all. Once Sonny finds out who you are, you sure as hell will be dead."

"He doesn't have to know."

"How could you say that, Clint? Don't most folks recognize you on sight?"

"Sure, they think they do. And when they ask me, I tell them they're right. I don't change my name, no matter how much easier it would be."

"But come on. People know your face. Gunmen know you even better and Sonny Byrnes is a gunman as well as a robber. Don't you forget it."

"I won't forget it," Clint said. "Believe me. But you'll have to trust that I know what I'm doing and can make this work. Sonny's real good at keeping his head down when he needs to, so tracking him will take too much time. What I need is to get in close as one of his kind. That way, he won't be so worried about hiding."

Frank shook his head. "I don't know about this. I don't think it's too good of an idea. You may be right about everything so far, but I don't want you to risk your life on account of me. One man I knew is already in his grave and I don't want you in one as well."

"I appreciate the sentiment, Frank, but there's something going on beneath the surface of all of this. I can smell more than enough smoke, which tells me there's also a fire. This goes beyond Sonny Byrnes. Sonny is a robber and there's no money in robbing loads of lumber. That means someone must be paying him very well to rob those loads. A man like Sonny Byrnes doesn't come cheap."

Frank started fidgeting in his bed and kicking at the board near his feet as though he was trying to crack the frame. "I should go with you," he grumbled. Every kick brought a wince of pain and with every wince, he seemed to get more agitated. "As damn fool crazy it is, I should go with you. All you wanted was to check up on me and now you've got your mind set on this suicide mission."

Clint looked over to Layla a split second before she started walking over to check on her patient. One assuring motion was all he needed to give and the nurse was turning back to her current task. "You won't be getting out of this bed, Frank," he said, putting a calming hand on the older man's shoulder.

"The hell I won't! You're not my nurse."

This time, rather than pat the older man's shoulder, Clint put a little muscle into it and held Frank down so he couldn't get to his feet. "I need you to stay here, but that's not all I need from you."

Frank's struggling subsided and he looked up to Clint with genuine interest. "What're you talking about now?"

"What I need from you is information. First off, I need

to know who hired that shipment that you were driving when you were robbed."

"That's easy. It's Ken McPike's company that needed them supplies."

"Do you know what he needed them for?"

"Building something. That's all I know. Hell, Clint, I was just supposed to see that wagon got from one place to another."

"Fair enough. You know where I can find McPike?"

"He's got an office right here in town."

"Great. Now is there anything you can tell me about McPike?"

Frank settled back against his pillow and rattled off what few things he knew about the man who'd hired him. It was all pretty basic since Frank's only concern had been his pay, where to pick up the wagon and where to drop it off.

There was something that caught Clint's interest regarding McPike's biggest competitor. The man's name was Albert Conroy and the only reason that Frank knew he and McPike were practically sworn enemies was because just about anyone who'd talked to either man found out soon enough.

"I'm sure of that," Frank said in regards to the bad blood between the two businessmen. "So sure that I made damn sure that McPike didn't know I ran some shipments for Conroy as well. That alone might have been enough to cost me this job."

"Sounds like there's something there I can work with," Clint said. "Anything else?"

After thinking for a moment or two, Frank shook his head. "Nope. But if I shake anything loose, I'll let you know."

"Fine. Now there's bound to be some people coming to you and asking about me once I leave here. I made no effort to cover my tracks, so it won't be too hard for someone to know I was here if they wanted to find out.

"Also, there might even be some people circulating around town asking questions about me or the robbery," Clint said in a voice that was just loud enough for Frank to hear.

"I'll keep quiet. No need to worry about that."

"Your job is information, Frank. Remember? If anyone asks about me, you give them whatever information you want. Just make sure it's the wrong information. I can pull this off, but only so long as I can count on you to cover me. Got it?"

Frank nodded. It was uneasy, but a nod all the same. "I got it. I still say you're crazy, though. What makes you think you can get in with Sonny's boys anyhow? And even if you do, how will you find out anything that you don't already know?"

"Have a little faith, Frank. Haven't you ever heard of honor among thieves?"

THIRTEEN

The day passed without incident.

It was just another stretch of hours that ended when the sun went down. Once the shadows came out, the town of Green Leaf kept just noisy enough for folks to find the saloons as well as the town's supply of soiled doves who advertised on the balcony over a billiards hall.

As with any town, the business district seemed completely deserted once the bankers and investors packed up their papers and headed home. Green Leaf's business district was only half a block long and consisted of about three or four buildings at the most.

At least, that was what Clint had gathered during the daylight hours when he'd scouted the area.

With the sun nothing more than a memory and the stars overtaking the sky, Clint had plenty of darkness to conceal himself as he moved from one alley to another toward the building marked as the McPike Shipping Company. It wasn't the biggest building in the area, but it sure helped when the man Clint was looking for labeled his doorway with his name on a sign.

Clint looked around as he snuck one storefront closer to where he wanted to be. By the time he got close enough

53

to show up as a reflection on McPike's front window, Clint realized there was no reason for him to be taking such pains to be silent. There wasn't a body in sight and as far as he could tell, there wasn't a living soul on the whole street.

As far as his eyes could see, there was only darkness and shadows. Not one window was glowing with the light of a lantern and the only voice he could hear came from the saloon two streets away. Still, he wanted to make sure he had his privacy so he kept quiet anyhow. At the very least, it would make for good practice.

Even though his skills branched off in several different areas, Clint was no thief. He knew there were ways to pick a lock and was somewhat familiar with the mechanism, but not familiar enough to get through it like a professional. Besides, McPike was supposed to find out that he'd been robbed sooner rather than later.

Clint stepped up to the front door of McPike's building and tried the handle. It was worth a try, but apparently Green Leaf wasn't so small that everyone felt safe enough to leave their doors open. Next to the door was a large front window. The window was actually one large pane of glass framed over several smaller ones.

The smaller panes were all about a foot square and precisely what Clint had been hoping to find. After one more quick glance around the street, Clint took off his hat and turned to face the front window. He placed the top of his hat against one of the smaller panes closest to the door and then tapped his fist into his hat.

The force of his punch was enough to shatter the small pane of glass and Clint's hat was strong enough to keep him from getting cut in the process. After dusting off his hat and placing it back upon his head, he used the handle of his Colt to clear out the broken shards of glass that remained in the little frame.

Since he was listening so intently for any sign of company, Clint's ears were still ringing with the muffled sound of breaking glass. That still wasn't enough to attract any unwanted attention, so he stooped down and reached his arm through the opening he'd created.

Just inside the window was a curtain that felt like dusty burlap against his knuckles. Clint reached past the edge of the curtain until he could feel the side of the front door. The broken pane was almost too low for him to feel anything but the door's jamb and the joints in his body began to bite at him with sharp jolts of pain from being twisted the wrong way.

Finally, Clint's fingertips found a handle and beneath that was the latch to unlock the door. He let out a relieved sigh when he was able to pull his arm out from the little opening. That relief was replaced by a sense of illicit pride when he pushed the door open and stepped inside the darkened office.

Once he was inside, Clint shut the door behind him and kept perfectly still so he could give his eyes a few moments to adjust. He'd been skulking about in the shadows for a while, but without the light of the stars or moon to guide him, the inky blackness closed in like a fist in a leather glove.

Before too much time had gone by, he could make out vague shapes in the dark. He knew that without some other source of light, he wasn't going to do much better than that so he started moving tentatively farther into the office. Clint walked slowly without lifting his feet much off the ground. That way, he could feel with the soles of his boots almost as much as he could with his roving hands.

Clint headed toward one blocky shape in particular and once he got there, he reached out to touch something smooth, curved and no bigger around than a thick branch.

Sure enough, there was a cool knob below the smooth curve which let Clint know that there was indeed a lantern on the desk directly in front of him.

He reached into his pocket to remove a match and only then realized how much easier it would have been to maneuver if he'd just struck that match as soon as he got inside. He shrugged and shook his head as he lit the match and then lit the wick of the lantern.

He may have gotten in like a thief, but he was still a long way from being a professional. There were worse things he could be than a bad thief.

Clint kept the lantern's flame down low and set it down on the floor behind a desk so no flickers would show in the window. From there, he went about the task that had brought him to the office in the first place. He searched through the biggest desks which he figured belonged to the most important people.

Now that he was out of plain sight, he got through locked doors with a strong shoulder or a well-placed kick. Just like the building itself, McPike's office was marked with the man's own name engraved on a plaque. Clint searched that office especially well and when he was done, there was no doubt that the place had been looted.

Clint surveyed the damage he'd caused as he headed for the front door. "If this turns out in McPike's favor," he thought as he snuffed out the lantern, "I'll pay for the repairs myself. If not, then he'll have a lot more to worry about than a few broken locks and a messy office."

FOURTEEN

Two weeks later, the air was getting cooler and the touch of winter could be felt like a hand that pressed down harder with every passing day. The days were getting shorter and every night was darker than the one before. It was just the way of things and nobody thought too much of it, even though a harsh winter could mean death.

People went about their lives not worrying about such dreadful things. Three such people were the men who rode on the wagon that was plodding along toward Mason's Pass, Arizona. They weren't worried about what the winter might bring. All they thought about was driving the wagon into Tombstone.

They weren't exactly carefree while going about their task. On the contrary, two of the men were armed and carrying their weapons for all to see. They'd hoped that would be enough to keep them safe and after the first few days had proven to be entirely boring, they figured they'd been correct. They carried their guns as if brandishing them was enough to frighten off any known threat. One had a Spencer rifle cradled in the crook of his arm and the other had a shotgun with the handle propped against his hip.

57

Even the driver seemed only partly aware of what he was doing. After all, they had enough time to get where they were going that the horses were allowed to go at their own pace. All the driver had to do was flick the reins to get them going at the start of a day and then pull back on them when the sun went down.

The men weren't exactly inept, but merely bored. That much showed in the tired droop of their eyelids as well as the drawl in their voices when they spoke to one another. They knew their jobs well enough. Some might say they knew their jobs a little too well since not one of them had the first suspicion that they would need to do more than just what they were doing.

The daylight was fading away and the sky was turning a comforting shade of red when the man with the Spencer rifle perked up enough to lift the rim of his hat away from his eyes. He set the rifle across his lap and used both hands to shield his eyes from the weak, yet persistent glare.

"What is it?" asked the man with the shotgun. "You see a place to stay for the night?"

The driver nodded lazily and said, "I sure hope so. My back feels like I was mule-kicked after camping on that rocky ground last night."

"Well it's your own damn fault for picking a spot that—"

"For Christ's sake just shut up," the man with the rifle said, cutting in on the other two. "The both of you, just keep quiet."

Instantly forgetting whatever they were going to say next, both the driver and the shotgunner turned to look in the same direction as their partner. All that could be seen at the moment was the shape of a figure on horseback surrounded by a cloud of dust.

"He's in a surefire hurry," the shotgunner said.

The rifleman, being the oldest of the three, squinted at

the figure and gritted his teeth. "Yeah. And he's headed this way."

Leaning forward in his seat, the driver asked, "Are you sure about that?"

"Yeah, I'm sure."

There was a moment where the only sounds that could be heard were the horses' plodding steps and the grinding of the wagon's wheels against the ground. That moment didn't even start to get tense before it was broken by the creak of the seat as the driver slumped back into his original position.

"Eh, it could be anyone," the driver said, giving the reins a small flick from lack of anything else to do. "Just as long as he don't want none of our coffee, I don't care who the hell he is. Them bitter grinds have been hard to come by lately."

The shotgunner stared out at the figure for another few moments. If he listened real hard, he could hear the low rumble of the distant horse's racing steps. Finally, he let out a breath and slumped back into his seat as well. "I told you we should've bought more coffee before we left, but you said we'd be fine with what we got."

"We should have been fine if you didn't drink so damn much."

Since the rifleman was concentrating on the road ahead, the other two men's chatter quickly faded into background noise. Something wasn't sitting too well with him and that feeling made him wrap his right hand around the rifle and slide his finger over the trigger.

His companions were too busy yammering on and on to notice, but the rifleman twisted around to get a look at the land around them. If he hadn't been looking for them specifically, he may very well have looked over the shapes of the other riders approaching in the distance.

There were two figures far off at the nine o'clock position as well as another pair at five o'clock. Those, along

with the rider coming at them nearly head-on, was enough
to make his grip around the rifle tighten even more.

Those others he'd spotted were still a ways off, but
that first rider was getting closer by the second. In fact,
that rider was so close that more details could be seen,
including the low position of his body against the horse's
back and the hand that was raised in the air to hold a
pistol over his head.

"Aw shit," the rifleman said. He lifted his weapon so
quickly that he knocked the shotgunner in the ribs.

"What the hell's got you so—" But the driver's question was cut off by the sharp crack of gunfire in the distance. He heard the sound and then saw the puff of smoke
which accompanied it, causing him to immediately grab
hold of the reins and steer away from the approaching
rider.

"Not that way!" the rifleman shouted when he saw they
were heading toward one of the other sets of riders. "The
other way! The other way!"

When the rifleman looked back to see what the closest
rider was doing, he was shocked to see that the oncoming
horse was going nearly twice as fast as he'd anticipated.
With his body running on reflex, he jammed the rifle
against his shoulder and squeezed off a shot.

After that, the fireworks really got started.

FIFTEEN

The rider bearing down on the wagon had only fired one more shot, but it still sounded like war had broken out on that trail. That was mostly due to the fact that once the two men on the wagon started shooting, they didn't take a rest until they had to reload their weapons. Even that pause didn't last long and soon the chaos was back in full swing.

In the space of another couple of seconds, that first rider was so close that everyone on that wagon could see the glint of the fading sunlight off the buttons of his duster. His horse was black as pitch and streaked right past them like a bolt of dark lightning.

"Holy shit!" the shotgunner said after he'd emptied both of his barrels. "Where'd he go?"

The question was answered by a jarring crash which caused the rusted springs beneath the front seat to groan and the entire wagon to tremble. That crash was the impact of two boots landing toward the front of the wagon's bed. Those boots belonged to the man who'd leapt off his horse as he rode by, still holding his pistol in one hand. The man's face was covered by a dirty bandanna which muffled the sound of his churning, powerful breaths.

The first one to react was the shotgunner. He twisted around in his seat and leveled his gun at the man who'd jumped onto the wagon. His finger pulled back onto both triggers, but he was rewarded with nothing but a dry clack as two hammers fell onto spent shell casings.

Ignoring the shotgunner, the masked man kept his body low and took one long step toward the front of the wagon. His feet moved deliberately beneath his body, maintaining his balance while the wagon jostled and bucked beneath him. As his other leg came forward, he snapped his boot out to kick the barrel of the rifle that was just coming around to bear on him.

The rifle went off as the barrel was kicked aside, sending a round through the air and well away from its intended target. Undaunted by the proximity of the shot or even the heat of the muzzle flash, the masked figure kept moving until he was within arm's reach of all three men at the front of the wagon.

Holding his upper body so low that the masked man seemed ready to throw himself into the driver's seat, he swung his gun hand forward, turning his fist sideways along the way. The swing ended with the handle of his gun smashing into the rifleman's fingers.

After that, the rifleman couldn't have hung onto his weapon if his life depended on it. And at that very moment, that certainly seemed to be the case. He was now looking down the barrel of the raider's pistol and for a moment, he was certain that the next thing he would lay eyes on was the face of God himself.

The raider moved like a flicker of lightning. As soon as the rifle started to drop, he reached out to catch it in his free hand. Shifting so he pointed the rifle at the man who'd previously been holding it, the raider snapped his pistol around to point directly into the shotgunner's face.

"Toss that shotgun aside," the raider commanded.

The shotgunner had a moment of bravery when he considered standing up to the other man, but that passed quickly enough. There was no chance in hell he could do more than twitch before the raider pulled his trigger. After swallowing that bitter pill, the shotgunner chucked his weapon over the side of the wagon.

Nodding, the raider took a step back and said, "Smart move. You, driver, pull this thing to a stop." When he saw his instructions weren't being carried out instantly, the raider shouted, "Now!"

The driver pulled back on his reins so hard that the horses nearly reared. Foam came from the animals' mouths as they were choked by the bits clamped in between their jaws. The wagon did rumble to a stop, however, and all three seated men waited nervously.

"All of you, get down from the wagon," came the command from the raider.

None of the three wanted to look back at the man that held a gun in each hand. They were doing well enough to keep from panicking and staring back into the masked face of their captor would only make things worse.

Sweat poured down from their faces as the three men did as they were told. They hopped down from the wagon and shifted on their feet. The two guards exchanged a few meaningful glances, but soon felt the touch of steel against their backs.

The raider's voice was tempered to a steely edge when he said, "I know both of you have backup guns. It'd be best if you toss them as well. I want the driver to unhitch the two front horses from that wagon."

"Look here, mister," the driver said. "There ain't nothing in this wagon you could want. It's just some—"

"Shut up and unhitch them horses," the raider interrupted. "Or I may lose my patience altogether."

That was enough to set things in motion. The driver

got the front pair of horses freed from the team while both
guards emptied their holsters and even fished the hunting
knives from their belts.

When all of that was completed, the raider told them,
"Now I want you three men to get on those two horses.
I know bareback ain't the most comfortable way to ride,
but it's either that or I plant you all right here. What'll it
be?"

The question was hardly in the open before the three
men were scrambling to mount the horses. Being the one
with the busted fingers, the rifleman was the one left
standing after the other two had chosen their rides. It was
the driver who leaned down to offer his help to let the
rifleman climb up behind him.

"Good," the raider said. "Now you three ride on in the
direction you were headed. If I see even one eye so much
as look back at me, I'll put a round through it. Understand?"

The three nodded, but kept their faces pointed away
from the masked man.

"That's fine. Now get the hell out of here before I
change my mind."

All three of them nearly fell off their horses when they
got them going, but their grips were ironclad and sheer
desperation allowed them to gain speed in no time.

Once the two horses were away, the raider glanced
around at the other two groups that were closing in on the
stopped wagon. He gave a short whistle and his own black
horse came trotting up to his side. Reaching into one of
the saddlebags, he removed a spyglass and pointed it at
each of the groups in turn.

There was no question about it. Both groups were riding at full gallop now and would reach the wagon in a
few minutes or less. Now that he had the spyglass, he
spotted something else as well. The approaching riders

were not coming in pairs, but were coming in two rows riding side by side.

It was an old trick to confuse trackers about how many were truly riding in their party, but it was an effective trick nonetheless. The raider nodded when he saw the approaching groups' formation. Just seeing that little bit was enough to tell him a little more about who he was dealing with.

The raider lowered the spyglass and reached up to pull the bandanna away from his face. Once he softened his expression and allowed the scowl to fade from his mouth, Clint looked more like himself. The dirt on his face was smudged on in thick coats and a few fresh cuts made him look even more scruffy.

Overall, the disguise was another simple trick that should work well enough. At least, he hoped it worked. Otherwise, his visit with the approaching riders might end up much differently than he wanted.

SIXTEEN

Clint climbed into Eclipse's saddle and sat with the rifle across his lap. He resembled the rifleman who'd been riding on the wagon to begin with and Clint knew this because he'd been watching the wagon ever since he caught up with it a day ago. A little research had told him that this was the only wagon in the area carrying a load similar to the ones that had been robbed.

Well, finding the correct wagon had taken a bit more than research. There had been a hell of a lot of luck involved as well.

The shotgun was left on the driver's seat. Since the owner of that weapon seemed to have taken his spare shells with him, Clint had no more use for the gun himself. Still, he left the empty shells in place and placed the weapon in a somewhat out-of-the-way location.

As he watched the other two groups converge on his location, Clint situated himself inside the shell he'd formed around himself since his real name wouldn't serve him too well in this situation. He didn't need much, since the less there was to remember, the less there was to mess up. Along the way, he'd come up with a few things to say about himself that wouldn't require much by way of proof.

What little proof he did need, he could simply borrow from the men he'd come across over the years. If his memory of the men he'd been forced to kill were good for anything, it was in supplying him with facts that nobody was in any shape to refute. Their faces still haunted him sometimes when he slept, as they would any man with a conscience. Clint figured he might as well put them to work.

As for his own face, Clint knew he was well enough known in some circles for that to be a problem. Plenty of men recognized him on sight. Actually, most of those men were almost certain they recognized him. That certainty was confirmed with a bit of checking and asking around and since Clint rarely hid himself, that was usually enough.

This time was an exception, however. To keep folks on their toes, Clint had taken to keeping his face dirty, which had a way of making any man look wilder and less like himself. He'd also adopted an expression that twisted his features just enough to make him look even more different.

To top things off, he'd cut his hair close to the scalp using nothing but his own Bowie knife. That, alone, altered his appearance significantly enough so that he could hardly recognize himself in his own shaving mirror. To that end, Clint's face hadn't felt a razor since the last time he'd spoken to Frank Zeller in Green Leaf. After the last week, there was enough stubble on Clint's cheeks and chin to obscure his features as well as cover the scar on his left cheek almost completely.

In a strange sort of way, Clint was proud of his transformation. He'd done a lot in little time and all of it led up to this very moment. He could hear the approaching hooves pounding against the ground like a steady roll of thunder moving through the air. His own heart quickened in his chest as he anticipated what might happen when the inevitable confrontation finally came.

On one hand, he was confident enough in himself to know that he could pull off the plan he'd formed. After all, if he didn't think he could do it, Clint wasn't about to try to follow through. As a gambler, he knew the difference between a risky bet and an impossible one. Knowing that difference often separated the great card players from the broke ones.

On the other hand, it had been quite a while since the last time he'd tried walking in another man's shoes. Doing so for the purpose of understanding that man was one thing, but making up that other man entirely was another. When dealing with a group led by the likes of Sonny Byrnes, one slip could be all it took for things to go really badly really quickly.

And that one slip could very well be the mistake to cost Clint his life.

The riders were getting closer. Although Clint could hear their voices as they shouted back and forth to one another, he couldn't quite make out what was being said. He didn't need to understand every word, however, to get the meaning behind them.

They were not happy. Not one bit. Of that much, Clint could be certain.

He smirked to himself at that thought, which seemed to be one hell of an understatement.

Even from this distance, Clint could feel the hostility coming from the riders and could hear as much in their gruff, angry voices. Now that they were close enough to see him better as well, they whipped their horses even harder to close the distance faster. The sound of cracking leather and snorting animals added a brutal spice to the noise in the air.

Slipping back into the facial expression he'd adopted for this disguise, Clint furrowed his brow slightly and squinted his eyes. He let his posture slouch a bit as well and by the time the riders were slowing and circling around him, he felt as though he was as much in character as he was likely to get.

Shifting his eyes more than his head, Clint surveyed the riders around him. There were nine in all and every last one of them had their guns drawn. All but two of them glared at him as if they wanted to kill him and gut him right then and there. Those two looked at him more cautiously. Luckily for Clint, those were the two that seemed to be leading the entire group.

Clint recognized one of the leaders as Sonny Byrnes. It hadn't been difficult at all to find a wanted poster with the man's face drawn on it. That, along with his own memory of the last time he'd tried to track down the robber, was enough for Clint to recognize him now.

Sonny still had the chiseled features and jutting nose that he'd had when his oldest posters had been drawn. His skin was olive hued with pockmarks scattered here and there between the plentiful scars. The beard and mustache were new in Clint's eyes. Most of the whiskers were oily black, but there were several streaks of silver shot through as well.

The face of the other one in charge didn't ring any bells in Clint's mind. He had a youthful appearance and sharp, cruel eyes. Slightly rounded cheeks took away a few years from his looks, but the coldness in those eyes and the easy confidence with which he led put those years right back.

"All right, mister," the unknown leader said to Clint. "Give me one reason why I shouldn't have my men fill you full of holes for interfering with our business."

Clint's mind raced to come up with a response. Judging by the murderous stares coming at him from all directions, he had to make sure it was damn good.

SEVENTEEN

"Interrupted yer business?" Clint asked. "And just what business is that?"

The man who'd asked the question stared across at Clint as though he didn't quite know what to make of him. "Our business was taking that shipment. Something tells me you already knew that."

"Maybe I did and maybe I didn't. Either way, as far as I can tell, I didn't interrupt a thing. Saved you some trouble, that's to be sure, but that's about it."

One of the other men in the group spat a juicy wad onto the ground and leaned forward in his saddle. "Let me put one right between his eyes, Jer. We've heard enough out of this asshole already."

One thing Clint didn't have to put any thought into was the deadly glare that he showed to the overly anxious gunman. All it took was a shift in his brow and a slow turn of his eyes to fix them upon his target and Clint could suddenly feel the burning swell up inside of him. Normally, he didn't like to make such an angry display. Doing so was a way of tipping your hand when gambling and more often than not accomplished nothing. But he was walking in a different circle now, and Clint was well aware that the rules had changed.

He was among the animals now and the occasional baring of teeth wasn't only expected, but necessary.

In a matter of seconds, the gunman who was aching to pull his trigger felt the heat of Clint's stare and backed down reflexively. He seemed annoyed at his own reaction since it had caused him to retreat in front of his own pack members.

The silent exchange was noticed by everyone in the group. Most of the others were anxious to jump in on their friend's behalf, but the two leaders merely watched with interest. Just as things were about to take on a life of their own, the man Clint didn't recognize once again stepped in to take the reins for himself.

"Ease it back, Ike. Nobody's gonna shoot anyone unless I say so. Is that understood?" When he didn't get an answer right away, he shot his own glance to the anxious gunman which calmed Ike down faster than a smack across the face. "I said, is that understood?"

Cowed, Ike lowered his eyes and sat back into his saddle. "Yeah, Jer. I understand."

All this time, Clint made sure to try and keep his eyes on as many of the gang members as possible. Since he didn't want to appear too uncomfortable, he didn't shift around in his saddle. That meant the men behind him stayed out of his sight and although that wasn't the best of situations, it was just the way it needed to be for the moment.

"As for you," the leader said, shifting his eyes back toward Clint. "You've got just enough of my interest to stay alive for another couple of seconds. Just who the hell are you anyway?"

With each second that passed, Sonny Byrnes was star-

ing at Clint intensely. "I think we run across each other
before. That right?"

Clint shrugged. "Could be. You're Sonny Byrnes,
right?"

Sonny nodded just enough for the movement of his
head to be seen. With his eyes fixed on Clint, the nod
seemed almost disconcerting.

"I've done some work in New Mexico and as far west
as California," Clint went on to say. "I come from the
Dakotas before that. Maybe we crossed paths there."

Sonny thought it over quietly. He was so quiet, in fact,
that he seemed to have wandered out of his own mind for
a second or two before his lips cracked apart and he said,
"Could be."

At this point, Clint was almost completely certain that
the man Ike had called Jer was the one at the head of the
gang's table. He was the one who set the pace for every
exchange and the others only seemed to talk as long as
he let them.

Jer had a vaguely amused smile on his face as he studied Clint carefully. "You never answered my question,"
he said. "Tell me who you are."

"My name's Matt Hendershott," Clint answered.

"And what brings you out here today, Matt Hendershott?" Jer asked. "Why are you so interested in this
wagon?"

"Simple," Clint responded. "I'm interested in it because you are."

That was just the kind of thing Ike had been waiting
for and he jumped on the opportunity the way a cat
jumped onto a mouse. "See there? He's tryin' to butt in
on our hit. Just let me put him down so we can take this
wagon and be on our—"

"I won't tell you again, Ike," Jer said without taking
his eyes from Clint. "Shut . . . up."

Ike started to protest, but it was Sonny who made him

think twice about it. The snarl on the infamous robber's face was full of so much cruel intent that even the men on either side of Ike winced at the sight of it. After seeing that, Ike shut his mouth and kept it shut.

"I'm waiting," Jer said to Clint.

"I got the shipping manifest from Ken McPike's office. I been hearing about these robberies and heard that Sonny over there was involved. I did a little scouting and figuring on my own and decided this would be the best place to find you."

"How'd you know this wagon would be hit?" Jer asked. "There must be dozens of these things rolling across the states where we've been working."

"I didn't know for sure. I've been following wagons like these for a while, waiting for one to get hit. I didn't move in until I saw you and your men closing in."

"And you thought this was a smart thing to do?"

"Yes, sir. I wanted to get your attention."

"Well, you got it. Now the question is, why you'd want it so badly?"

"I'm a hard worker and a damn good thief. I figured anyone working with the likes of Sonny Byrnes would be a good place for me to make some good money. And I thought that the only way for you to know that would be to see my work for yourself."

Jer nodded to himself and glanced toward the horizon. The shapes of the two horses carrying the wagon's guards and driver could still be seen, but were no more than dots shrinking in the distance.

"What about them?" he asked. "Why'd you let them live?"

Clint looked at the dots on the horizon and shrugged. "I'm a robber and good in a fight, but I don't need to be wanted for murder. That is, not unless I've got the backing of a good gang behind me."

"All right then. Prove it." Pointing to the dots in the

distance, Jer said, "Run those men down and kill all but one. I don't care which one gets to live, but only one does, got it? And I want you to do it quickly. A slow gun hand's no use to anyone, especially me."

"And if I do?" Clint asked. "What's in it for me?"

"You get a chance with me and my boys here and the backing you were talking about. Mess this up and you won't live to see the sunset. Go."

Clint turned Eclipse toward the retreating horses and snapped the reins. The Darley Arabian took off like he'd been shot from a cannon and in no time at all, Clint was listening to the mad rush of wind pouring past his head.

"Go with him, Dell," Jer said to one of the other gunmen nearby after Clint had left. "See that he does his job right and if he doesn't, kill him. We've wasted enough time on him already."

EIGHTEEN

Clint allowed himself a little smirk as he bolted away from the gang of robbers led by Sonny Byrnes and the other one called Jer. So far, Jer's face still didn't strike any chords in Clint's mind, but that might change once he found out the man's full name. In the meantime, however, he had more immediate concerns.

He didn't have to look back to know that he was being followed. Clint could hear the distant rumble of hoof beats behind him and could feel the eyes of the other rider like two pokers on his back. He knew he was running a major risk by taking off after the men he'd let go before. The first of those risks was of being shot in the back as soon as he took off.

Something in Clint's gut told him that wasn't going to happen, though. If Jer or Sonny had wanted him dead, it was more likely they would have shot him down before where all their men could see it up close. But more than that, Clint had spotted something in Jer's eyes that was the source of the smirk now upon Clint's face.

Like any poker player worth his salt, Clint could read the signs his opponents gave off. He could even read the ones an opponent didn't know they were giving off since those were the ones that could make or break any high-stakes hand.

Jer was buying into what Clint was feeding him.

Sonny was a bit harder to read and seemed naturally more cautious, but Jer was buying into it. If he wasn't, Clint figured he would be dead, wounded, or still shooting it out with the entire gang at that very moment. Instead, he was being tested and watched like a hawk.

That was more than enough to give Clint hope, but he knew damn well that he was a long way from getting out of the woods just yet.

Both of the horses that had been liberated from the wagon's team were past their prime and tired as hell. The men riding them, on the other hand, were desperate and running for their lives. That meant the guards and driver had an impressive lead after the several minutes that had passed since Clint had let them go.

In fact, if they'd been on better horses, the three men might have been out of Clint's reach. As it was, they were a ways off, but not too much so for Clint to be unable to catch them. In a way, Clint felt bad for putting those men through the hell they'd had to endure. Of course, growing a few more gray hairs in one day was a hell of a lot better than one of them crawling to the next town after watching his other two friends get killed in front of him.

It would have made Clint feel much better if he'd had more than the bare bones of a plan to deal with those three and still maintain his disguise. But since his instincts had carried him this far fairly well, he decided to keep trusting them and follow through on what little bit of a plan he had.

The first part of that plan involved the man who was surely behind him. Once he'd put some distance between himself and the wagon where most of the gang was waiting, Clint took a quick look over his shoulder. Just as he'd figured, there was indeed someone following him. Luckily, there was only one.

Turning to face front once again, Clint guessed the two horses carrying the three poor fellows that were the wagon's original crew hadn't spotted him just yet. They were too far ahead to see much more than basic shapes, but they were still riding in the same direction at roughly the same speed.

The other gang member was about ten or fifteen yards behind him and gaining on him slowly but surely. Clint gave Eclipse a subtle instruction using the reins and positioned himself in just the right spot between the horses in front and the one behind him.

Clint didn't have to look again to figure how much closer the man following him was getting. A few seconds more, he guessed, and the robber would be right where Clint wanted him. Any longer than that, and he would be too close for his next play to work as well as he wanted.

The seconds ticked by and Clint counted off each one of them in his head. He could hear the horse drawing up closer behind him, its hooves pounding at a furious pace. Soon, he could start to hear the powerful breaths of the animal and the urgent commands of its rider as the robber snapped his reins and hunkered down for the ride.

Just another few seconds, Clint thought.

His eyes were now solidly locked onto the horses ahead of him. Although there was still plenty of distance to cover, he was closing it pretty well.

Behind him, the other horse was close enough for Clint to feel the rumble of its steps in the ground. For an experienced rider, everything from the sounds and sights around him to the tremors he could feel though his legs and hands were important. Each of them showed Clint a little piece of a larger picture.

This picture was coming into focus by the second and

when it finally did, he saw the exact moment he'd been waiting for.

He didn't have to say a word. All Clint had to do was snap Eclipse's reins and touch his heels to the stallion's sides to give the Darley Arabian permission to charge into a full-out run. All this time, Clint had been riding fast enough to make it appear that he was going as fast as he could. The idea was to keep up appearances while also tiring out the horse that was behind him.

Judging by the way the sound of the trailing horse faded away, Clint knew his gamble had worked. Now he could cover some serious ground with enough time to get to the other two horses well before any of the gang could reach them.

Eclipse's breath came in bursts as powerful as a steam engine. His head surged forward and back as his hooves practically floated over the ground. The stallion was running so fast that his back hardly moved up or down. All his motion was flowing forward and all Clint had to do was hold on for the ride.

The rider that had been following Clint was nothing more than a memory which became hazier with every passing second.

NINETEEN

Although it was difficult to focus his eyes while clutching onto the back of a runaway train, Clint could see enough of the riders ahead of him to know that he'd been spotted. Actually, the guards and driver would all have to have been deaf and blind to not figure out that someone was chasing them down.

Clint could see the horses wobble slightly in their path as the riders tried to figure out which way they should run. Since they were in the middle of an open trail with nothing but scrub and bushes nearby, their options were decidedly limited. But even so, they weren't about to give up and eventually both of the horses turned toward a hill that was at least a mile away.

Shaking his head, Clint had to give the guys credit for trying. Especially since Clint and Eclipse must have looked like death itself to men who'd already been through hell and thought they'd made it out alive. But there was no way around that for the time being. In fact, Clint knew he was actually doing the men a big favor.

Eclipse seemed to know that he was chasing after the other two horses by this point and when he got a little closer to them, he would strain that much harder. With so

little space left to cover, Clint allowed the Darley Arabian
to keep pushing himself until they were within five to ten
yards away.

Every couple of seconds, one of the three men ahead
of Clint would turn and look at him. When they looked
back, it was with a terrified expression on their face and
desperation in their voices. They kicked their horses even
more until their legs were trembling from the strain. But
before too long, the wagon horses had given all they could
give and no amount of coaxing would change a thing.

Even from where he was, Clint could see the moment
the two horses had reached their limits. Like a train that
had blown a piston, the horses started shimmying and
making more noise while slowing down to a grinding halt.

The guards and driver were shouting curse after curse
at the animals, but to no avail. Eventually, they had to
just accept the inevitable and turn to face what was coming. When they got a look at what was behind them, they
dropped from the horses' backs and hit the ground running.

Their eyes went wide as saucers when they saw Clint
bearing down on them like a one-man stampede. The
guards fumbled at their holsters only to find them empty.
The driver started to run in one direction, but quickly
turned and ran toward the hill instead.

Watching the three men scramble like chickens with
their heads lopped off, Clint couldn't help but find the
scene amusing. He hated to admit it, but the way the trio
tripped over themselves and their horses to sprint for a
hill that was still the better part of a mile away was just
funny. He didn't allow those thoughts to be reflected on
his face, however. Instead, he wore a mask of pure stone.

His eyes went cold and his lips parted slightly to bare
his teeth like the animal he was pretending to be.

Clint pulled back on Eclipse's reins as the stallion
thundered toward the three men and the horses they'd

abandoned. Amazingly enough, the Darley Arabian didn't seem to be out of steam just yet and it took an effort on Clint's part to convince the animal to slow down.

Eclipse responded to Clint's commands soon enough and came to a shuddering stop only slightly past the other three men. As soon as he was able, Clint swung down from his saddle and drew his Colt the moment his boots hit the dirt. Using his own momentum, he rushed toward the closest man which was the driver who'd been attempting to make a run for it on his own.

With the precision of a surgeon, Clint aimed and fired in the space of a heartbeat. The Colt barked once and bucked against his palm, spitting out its round which dropped the driver down to one knee.

The driver let out a groan that was filled with more frustration than pain as he struggled to get moving, but fell onto his stomach instead. The bullet had scraped his leg, doing as much damage as a set of angry fingernails. He rolled onto his back with his arms flailing at the ground when he came face to face with the man who'd put him there.

Clint was breathing heavily after his run and stood over the wagon driver, staring down at him with his Colt in hand. Before he did anything else, however, he took a quick glance up at the other horse that was quickly approaching.

That was all the driver needed to make a play of his own and swiped out for one of Clint's feet with his closest hand. His fingers only closed on empty air, however, since Clint had lifted his leg in plenty of time to avoid the clumsy grab.

Seeing that their partner had been overtaken, both the guards were running toward Clint. The panic and desperation had overtaken them and Clint knew he would have to act first and talk later. He acted in a fraction of a second, shifting his aim and picking shots so precise that he even had to take the wind factor into account before pulling the trigger.

Clint took two more shots in quick succession, dropping the shotgunner first and rifleman second. Both men went down awkwardly, landing in a crumpled heap on the ground and sporting wounds similar to the driver's. Neither of them stopped flailing until Clint ran over to them and pointed his Colt squarely in their faces.

Knowing he only had less than a minute before the man following him would arrive, Clint kept his voice sharp and clear. He stared down the modified pistol and said, "Both of you listen up, because I can only say this once."

After Clint spoke his piece, he went over to the driver and said it again. When he was done, the other robber was bearing down on their position but slowing up a bit. Apparently, he wanted to see what Clint was about to do.

By now, the guards and driver were lying on their stomachs with their hands behind their backs. Not wanting to disappoint his audience, Clint straightened up, sighted down the Colt's barrel and fired one round into the back of each guard's head. The driver took one in the ribs and the blood of all three men soaked into the gritty earth beneath their bodies.

TWENTY

Dell was a slender kid who'd been riding with Sonny and Jer for only a few months or so. In that time, he'd seen more than enough to open his eyes to the new life he'd chosen. He'd seen plenty of blood and had shot his fair share of men. But when he rode up on the stranger and the three men he'd chased down, he couldn't help but be surprised.

"I'll be damned," Dell said when he saw the still bodies and the blood flowing from their heads. "You didn't even wait for me to get here."

Still holding the smoking Colt in his hand, Clint let his eyes linger on the bodies of the two guards at his feet in a way he'd seen killers soak up the sight of their work. Even he could feel the icy chill in his gaze when he turned it toward the younger man on horseback.

"Was I supposed to wait?" Clint asked.

"No. I suppose not." Dell looked toward the driver, who had just been grazed by the gunshot and now was fleeing for his life. "What about him?" he asked.

"I was supposed to let him go."

"But he looks hurt."

"He took a bullet in the side to slow him down. I figured it'd be a good reminder for what he saw here today. I didn't get the impression I was supposed to just let him skip out of here unscathed."

"No, you weren't," Dell said, unable to keep himself from looking once again at the two bodies that remained.

The simple truth of the matter was that Dell had fired his gun when his life depended on it. He was a hell of a robber and had the sand to walk through his fair share of fire, but what he'd just seen didn't sit too well with him.

Clint recognized the look floating behind the kid's eyes. It was something he hadn't quite expected, but was very glad to see. It was a conscience, and it wasn't doing the kid any favors at the moment. No doubt, that had been why the kid had been sent to check up on him.

If Clint hadn't pulled his trigger, then Dell surely had been ordered to pick up the slack. And if the job had been done satisfactorily, then it gave the kid a chance to feast his eyes upon the uglier side of the life he'd chosen.

For Clint, that short moment was very important. He stowed it away in the back of his mind, but didn't let his face reflect more than the slightest of thoughts. His eyes were still blank. His face remained unreadable.

A flawless poker face.

The perfect disguise.

"What's the matter, kid?" Clint asked. "You never seen dead men before?"

Dell wiped away his true expression as best he could and puffed out his chest. His hand dropped to his holster and he stuck a jagged edge onto his voice. "I seen plenty of dead men, don't you worry. I'll be lookin' at one more if you don't get back onto that horse of yours and come on back with me."

Kneeling down to the shotgunner's prone body, Clint reached for the scabbard on the side of his boot and removed a thin throwing knife. Lowering the knife to the shotgunner's bloody scalp, he asked, "You think your boss would want a little keepsake?"

"He don't like to be kept waiting. Just get on your horse and come with me."

Clint nodded and sheathed his blade. The only reason he'd asked that last question was because he knew what the answer was going to be. Sure enough, Dell's face had paled somewhat when Clint made his gruesome intentions clear. He knew Jer and Sonny would hear about it, which would add a little more credibility to the character that Clint was playing.

When Dell brought his horse around to face back toward the wagon and the gang waiting there, Clint walked over to Eclipse and climbed into the saddle. All the while, he did his best to keep himself and the Darley Arabian between Dell and the bodies. That way, at least the kid would have a hard time seeing the guards shaking.

The rumble of hooves faded away to a dull roar. Then, it quieted to a thumping in the distance until finally the guards on the ground could only hear it because their ears were so close to the earth. Even then, they were afraid to get up. Once those fears receded, their bodies were almost too weak to respond anyway.

"Hey," the rifleman whispered.

He got no response.

"Hey. You alive?"

The shotgunner tried to say something, but his words were choked in his throat. Finally, he managed to get out, "I'm alive. Damn near pissed myself, but I'm alive. Should we get up?"

"No. He said we should wait until we hear the whole gang ride away."

"Yeah, and he also said he wouldn't hurt us, but that was before he said he was gonna scalp me. Did you hear that?"

"Hush up," the rifleman said in a sharp whisper. "He wasn't gonna scalp you. If he wanted to hurt us, he would'a done it when he shot us." Reaching back to touch the bloody wound on his head, the man winced and let out a breath. "I can't believe he did that," he whispered. When he lifted his head slightly, he could see the deep little hole that had been dug by Clint's bullet after slicing though the skin over his ear.

The shotgunner was looking at a similar hole near his own head. "I know. That son of a bitch is crazy."

"The hell he is. He's the best damn shot I ever even heard of. He said he was gonna have to make it look like we was dead and that he had to shoot us to make it look that way."

"Yeah, well he could've shot a little farther away. My head's bleeding so much, my hair's sloppy with it."

Settling back down into his previous position, the rifleman said, "That was the idea. Cuts on yer head bleed like hell. Even the shallow ones. We'll be fine."

"Maybe. What about Ed? He's running with a wound in his side and may not even make it to—"

"The wound was a scratch on his ribs. Hell, I bet that bullet didn't even make it through the blubber around his belly."

The shotgunner dropped back down as well. Even though he'd only lifted himself an inch or so, he dropped like a rock and let out a disgruntled breath when he hit. "He didn't have to do all that to us, though. What if he missed?"

"Stop with yer bellyaching already. You sound like a goddamn baby. I don't know who that fella was or why he saved us, but I know we was supposed to be dead and he saved our lives. Just because we got to walk back with a cut and some bloody hair, you're not gonna hear me complaining. Now just do what you were told, shut up and sit still until them others leave."

Both guards shifted back into roughly the same position that they'd been in after getting the grazing shots over their ears. The blood was still trickling from the wounds, which made them more uncomfortable than the occasional pricks of pain they felt from the superficial cuts.

"I still say that son of a bitch is crazy," the shotgunner muttered. "A hell of a shot . . . but crazy."

TWENTY-ONE

Another thing Clint knew he could count on was Dell
trying to regain some of his own pride during the ride
back to the wagon. Although Clint hadn't been thinking
along those lines when he'd left him in the dust before,
it only made sense that the kid was smarting after having
been smoked by Eclipse so soundly on their way to where
the guards were waiting.

Competitiveness. It was yet another frailty of youth
that could so easily be twisted around to a smart player's
advantage.

Sure enough, after a few moments of easy riding, Dell
spurred his horse along just enough so he could be in the
lead. Clint let the kid have his small victory and took the
opportunity to take another look back at the guards.

As far as he could tell, both men were staying still and
following orders. He knew they were all right because
he'd subtly checked on them before and after he'd shot
them. Without reaching around too much to pat himself
on the back, he couldn't help but be just a little proud of
those two shots he'd taken. Although they hadn't been
nearly as rushed as they'd appeared, both shots to the
guards' heads had been masterpieces.

Clint had shaved off just enough flesh to get the blood flowing without causing too much damage. He knew a messy head shot was the only way for him to fake those men's deaths in a hurry. If his aim had been off even a fraction of an inch one way, all he would have gotten was a hole in the dirt. Too far in the other direction and he would have done the job for real.

Those shots may have been masterpieces, but Clint wasn't looking to replicate them anytime soon.

The kid was starting to pull ahead a bit more and then he pulled back on his reins instead. It seemed he'd nearly forgotten that he was supposed to escort Clint and not race him. Glancing back, Dell motioned for Clint to move up beside him.

After that, they rode the rest of the way together. All the while, Clint saw that Dell's hand never broke contact with his weapon. There was a wariness in his eyes regarding Clint as well. There was just a bit of fear, but it was tempered and controlled.

Clint read those eyes just fine. The kid wasn't so much scared of him as he was rattled by what he thought was cold-blooded murder that had been dealt as quickly as a snake's bite.

Good, Clint thought. *Just be sure to tell your friends.*

Dell didn't say much on the ride back. In fact, he didn't even say a word. He forced himself to keep Clint in his sight. It was all he could do to keep from drawing his gun for no reason. Clint knew the kid was thinking he had a real good reason to draw that gun. He knew because he had put that reason in the kid's head.

Like a master bluffer in a high-stakes game, Clint was plying his art every second of every day and that had started the moment another man had laid eyes on Matt Hendershott.

Before starting in on this task, Clint had done a bit of research back in Green Leaf. So far, there had been almost

a dozen robberies much like the one that had put Frank
Zeller in that infirmary. And for every man who'd wound
up like Frank, there were at least two others who'd wound
up like Frank's partner.

High stakes, indeed, and Clint was in it until the end.

He knew first-hand that Sonny Byrnes would be too
hard to track down the old-fashioned way. In the time it
took to find him, other men would have been killed. And
even if he was found, riding up to him with a posse in
tow would have only resulted in a bloody shoot-out where
Sonny might wind up escaping anyhow.

No, Clint had known that he needed to take the sneak-
ier path from the beginning. There was more going on
than just robberies. Clint had known that the instant he'd
read that story in the newspaper. Although he wasn't any
kind of crusader, Clint wasn't the type who liked to sit
back and let killers roam free and hunt like they had a
license.

All of that had brought him this far and now it was
too late for him to turn back. He was in this now, for
better or worse, whether he liked it or not.

As they approached the wagon, Dell looked over to
Clint and signaled for him to slow down. "Go on over,"
he said, pointing to where both leaders were waiting.

"All right," Clint said with grim resolve. "I'm ready."

TWENTY-TWO

By the time Clint and Dell were back where the wagon had been left, Jer had already gotten his men to replace the missing horses from the team with two of their own. Those two riders were the ones climbing onto the driver's seat and preparing the wagon to roll.

Watching the two come in from dealing with the original wagon's crew, Jer was beaming with good will. He looked like a man who'd won every hand at a full night's game of poker and he literally greeted Clint and Dell with open arms.

"I heard the shots," Jer said. Looking to Dell, he asked, "How'd he do?"

Dell had managed to bury the haunted look that had been in his eyes and merely nodded when he said, "Fine. He let the driver go."

"Healthy?"

"No. Shot him in the ribs."

A look of mild concern came over Jer's face. "But he'll make it, right?"

"Sure, he should make it."

"Good. What about the guards?"

That haunted look was creeping back into Dell's face.

91

No matter how hard he tried, he just couldn't shake it. "Dead. Both of them."

While the kid seemed to be having a hard time digesting what he'd seen, Jer couldn't be happier to hear the news. His smile actually broadened and he finally faced Clint head on. Up to this point, he'd talked to Dell as if Clint hadn't even been there. Now, not only did the gang leader seemed to take notice of Clint, but he looked at him like a long lost buddy.

"You did a fine job, Matt," the leader said.

For a moment, Clint didn't respond to the other name he'd taken on. But that only came as a twinge in the back of his mind and didn't show on his face in the slightest.

Not noticing one bit of difference, Jer went on to say, "It looks like you're a man who knows how to do his job. You took a big risk coming here and stepping ahead of us in robbing this wagon. You know how close you were to getting shot?"

Clint shrugged. "Yeah, but this wasn't the first time. I don't mind taking risks so long as the payoff justifies it."

Jer studied him for one more moment before clapping his hands together and reaching out to clasp Clint's hand. "I like you, Matt Hendershott. I wasn't exactly looking for anyone else to join up with us, but it'd be foolish to turn down someone as talented as you. What do you say, Sonny?"

The sullen robber was leaning against the wagon. He hadn't said a word since Clint and Dell had come back, but his eyes had been on both men the entire time. Now, he clenched his jaw as though he was chewing on his tongue and finally nodded.

"Sure," the robber said. "Why not? I could always kill him if he steps out of line."

Jer nodded as though the other man had just invited Clint to dinner instead of threatened his life. "True enough. Looks like it's unanimous then. Welcome to the gang, Matt. My name's Jeremiah Proffit."

This time, Clint had to fight hard to keep his expression from revealing the jolt that went through his system. He, along with most of the other peace officers west of the Mississippi, had heard of Jeremiah Proffit but never truly thought the man existed. Of course, this man could have been using the infamous name as a quick way to earn respect, but something in Clint's instincts told him that wasn't the case.

Despite Clint's best efforts, he must have let a change show in his expression because Proffit reacted to it with a knowing smile. "You've heard of me?"

"A bit," Clint said. "Just tall tales, mostly."

"Well, don't believe everything you hear. We can talk more later. For now, we best get this wagon rolling before anyone comes poking around here after all that shooting."

With that, everyone in the vicinity jumped to action. The two men on board the wagon flicked their reins and got the entire thing rumbling into motion. The remaining robbers climbed into their own saddles and took up positions around the wagon.

Dell snapped his fingers at Clint and motioned for him to ride up near the front of the wagon. Once there, Clint could feel the eyes of every man there boring straight between his shoulder blades. The sensation wasn't anything close to comfortable, but he put up with it anyway. When he took a quick look back, he could see only two horses remained behind.

Sonny Byrnes and Jeremiah Proffit were the men on those horses. They watched the wagon and all their men with casual indifference. Responding to Clint's backwards glance with a subtle nod, Proffit leaned over to Sonny and said something that only got a few nods in reply from the other robber.

Clint had heard of people who'd lost their hearing who were able to tell what was being said to them by reading lips. Although he could make out one or two words if he was watching someone through a spyglass, he didn't have the faintest idea what Proffit was saying to Sonny. Reading lips would have been a good skill to have at that moment, but since he didn't have it Clint turned around and faced front.

Clint felt the hairs stand up on the back of his neck and knew they wouldn't be coming down again until he was no longer at the head of this notorious group of robbers and killers. Although he'd been shot at plenty of times, now he truly knew what it felt like to be a clay pigeon in a shooting gallery.

Unfortunately, sitting quietly in that shooting gallery was all a part of the game that Clint was playing. The important thing was that he truly felt like he'd been accepted into the fold of murderers. At least, he'd been accepted for the time being.

If Proffit or Sonny hadn't trusted him, Clint would have been dead already. Of course, there was always the chance that one of them did recognize his face despite his efforts to hide it. Clint just needed to swallow that chance, sit in that shooting gallery and try to get out in one piece.

Some things, he knew, were easier said than done.

TWENTY-THREE

The gang rode along the same trail that the wagon had been using for another three miles before leaving it altogether. Mason's Pass cut through a rocky ridge that only rose about thirty or forty feet above ground level. The ridge was mostly dry, cracked rock covered with a thin layer of brush that had been made even thinner by the change of seasons from summer to autumn.

The trail they'd been following was wide enough for two wagons to pass each other with room to spare and it was easy to see by the mess of tracks underfoot that the path was well traveled. One of the robbers raced ahead and motioned for Clint to follow him away from the trail and toward the side of the ridge.

There were a few scraggly trees growing there with rocks the size of a man's head and bigger ones gathered around the roots. Once there, Clint was put to work clearing away the rocks and fallen branches. When this was done, he noticed that the trees weren't even growing out of the ground, but merely propped against a large fissure in the ridge wall. Although the propped up trees were definitely larger than most of the others nearby, they

95

didn't look so out of place that they would attract much attention.

Clint and the other robber cleared away the obstructions within a few minutes. By that time, the wagon had rolled up to the mouth of the fissure and was waiting to head inside. The opening was just wide enough for the wagon to get in, but it was a tight fit. The remaining gang members rode inside after the wagon, leaving Clint and the other man to cover up the opening once again.

The fissure was more than just a passage to some more secluded part of the pass. Clint looked down at the ground beneath Eclipse's hooves and saw well-worn ruts in the earth that were too deep for Proffit's gang to have put there. It must have been some old trail that had fallen out of use and that nobody really looked for anymore.

After several minutes of riding, Clint got a good idea why the trail was no longer favored by normal travelers. The ridge itself loomed over the path in a way that made him immediately suspect an ambush. No doubt, enough wagons and stagecoaches had been taken there that anyone with any knowledge of the area abandoned the path altogether.

On the other hand, for a gang of thieves, the path was more than perfect. Being the ones doing the ambushing, they could easily keep watch over the path with only a few men posted on top of the ridge. In fact, Clint only had to look up there for a minute or two before he spotted a figure looking back down at him from above. The figure appeared to be alone and watched the wagon with only passing interest. No doubt, if there were unwanted riders coming down that same path, an ambush could be quickly arranged.

The narrow trail wound back and forth and the ground itself angled at a downward slant. Finally, after nearly half an hour of slow riding, the group broke through the confines of the pass and into an open area that was surrounded on all sides by high, parched rock.

Clint shook his head and surveyed the area, which was a basin roughly circular in shape and under a quarter of a mile wide. There were wooden structures around the side of the basin that resembled watchtowers built in a fort. They were only big enough to hold one man, but there were enough of them to make anyone feel very safe in the camp below.

That camp was made up of several small shacks, plenty of tents and a few sturdier cabins. One of those cabins appeared to be a cookhouse, since that was the only one that gave off the slightest trickle of smoke. A rough guess put the population of the camp at a couple dozen, but there was no way for Clint to know how many more were in any of the structures.

He knew he was in the right place, however, when he looked toward a large corral containing plenty of horses as well as an unusual amount of empty flatbed wagons. The wagon that had been commandeered that day kept rolling straight toward the corral and the robbers spread out to head for one of the many tents or buildings. Before Clint could decide where he wanted to go first, he saw Proffit and Sonny steer away from the group and come over to ride on either side of him.

"So what do you think, Matt?" Proffit asked. "We've got our own little town here. The only thing you won't find is a sheriff's office."

"This is mighty impressive," Clint said earnestly.

Proffit nodded as though he expected the praise and said, "Come on. I'll give you a tour."

Clint followed the other man and looked back to see if Sonny was coming as well. The killer just sat in his saddle and looked on without moving an inch. There was something dangerous in his eyes when he watched Clint.

If it was uncertainty regarding a new member of the gang, Clint knew he could work around it.

If it was outright suspicion regarding Clint's story, then Clint knew he might not only be spending some time in that hidden town; he might wind up buried there.

TWENTY-FOUR

Clint's tour of the hidden town was short and sweet. Proffit led him around the perimeter and pointed out the places he would need to go for food and where to put up his horse. There was everything he could want in that basin including a blacksmith and a saloon.

As he was shown the area, Clint knew that he was spotted as an unfamiliar face by nearly everyone else who could see him. Even with Proffit riding beside him, Clint was getting no small amount of challenging stares and enough suspicion to give the air a bitter taste in the back of his throat.

Proffit ended up at a group of tents on the outskirts of the main buildings. "Here's where you sleep," he told Clint. "Find yourself an empty tent or someone willing to share and you're good as gold. There's food in the cookhouse and some in the saloon."

"Thanks, Mr. Proffit. I really appreciate this."

"Well, don't thank me yet. Sonny's still not too sure about you and just might kill you before tomorrow morning."

The way Proffit dropped that last statement, one might have thought he was discussing nothing more important than the weather. His expression remained friendly and his voice didn't even waver beyond his normal conversational tone.

Despite all of this, Clint had no doubt that Proffit was being completely honest with him in regards to the other robber. He could tell that much by the coolness in Proffit's eyes as well as the menace he'd read on Sonny Byrnes's face all day long.

"I won't disappoint you," Clint said.

"We'll just have to see about that, Matt. Get yourself settled, rested and fed and I'll find you when it's time to earn your keep." With that said, Jeremiah Proffit tipped his hat and rode toward the biggest cabin in the basin that wasn't in the main cluster.

Clint watched him leave and then looked around for Sonny. He couldn't find a single trace of Byrnes anywhere. There was no shortage of suspicious, hostile eyes looking in his direction, but Sonny's wasn't among them.

It was time to live up to his character, Clint knew. Not only did he have to convince the gang leaders that he was a criminal, but he had to live as one in order to survive. Clint knew enough about the world of killers and thieves to know that they lived like animals in a jungle filled with predators. Not only did they worry about the law, but they also had to concern themselves with staying alive in each other's company.

Clint had recognized that savage look in a killer's eyes, but now he had to do one better and put that look into his own. Feeling the primal cold swell up from his gut, Clint ignited the predatory fire within himself and turned that gaze toward the closest person he could find.

That man looked to be in his late forties and had the dirty face of a battlefield casualty. He'd obviously seen death before and had dealt it out plenty of times. It was also obvious that he didn't appreciate Clint being so close to him and he didn't try to hide it.

When Clint looked at that man, he not only pictured himself killing him but tried to convince himself that he wanted nothing more than to watch him die. Those thoughts, combined with Clint's own well-practiced glare had a definite impact on the other man. Although he didn't make a big show out of it, the nearby killer averted his eyes and walked away.

When Clint looked around for the next man who wanted to test him, there were no takers. In the criminal jungle, that was a victory in its own right. And even though he'd won it without too much difficulty, Clint wasn't looking forward to being on his toes twenty-four hours every day that he was among those men.

He had to sleep sometime. But Clint knew it wasn't going to be the least bit restful in the camp.

After leaving Eclipse in the corral and removing his saddle, Clint made his way over to the wagons that were lined up along one side of the fenced in space. As he moved toward the wagons, Clint looked around to see if he was being watched at the moment. The warning glance he'd given out earlier combined with the fact that he was in the middle of a horse pen allowed him a small window of privacy.

He didn't count on that privacy lasting for long, however, and fought back the urge to investigate right then and there. Just because he couldn't see that he was being watched, he knew that didn't mean someone wasn't watching him. The fact that he hadn't been in camp for an hour yet meant that Clint could pretty much count on being watched for a while.

When he turned back to walk out of the corral, he was glad he'd held off on scouting things out for the time being. Not only was he being watched, but there was a small group of men watching him from where they stood in front of the cookhouse. Clint waved to them and kept on walking.

TWENTY-FIVE

He didn't stop walking until he made it to the building designated as the camp's saloon. Actually, the place was a cross between a building and a tent since the walls were thick canvas supported by a wooden frame. Each wall had a few panels of wood here and there, making it seem as though the place had been stitched together using whatever material had been available at the time.

The door was made out of one of those panels and when Clint went to open it, he found the handle to be made out of a piece of thick rope looped through two holes in the wood. It swung open with a rusty shriek and slammed shut behind him after Clint had stepped inside.

Despite the fact that the place was situated in the middle of a basin within a town that didn't exist on any map, the saloon really wasn't too bad. Clint had visited plenty others in his day that were worse, but none that boasted of a more dangerous crowd.

The bar was on his left and appeared to have been made out of crates salvaged from alleyways and cargo shipments. The crates were held together with planks nailed along the side, creating one continuous, uneven surface that came up slightly higher than waist level. Behind the bar, there were stacks of boxes containing every kind of bottled liquor Clint could imagine. At the far end was where the kegs of beer and stacks of tin cups were kept.

Despite the fact that there were only about ten to thirteen souls in that ramshackle building, the saloon still managed to feel crowded. That was mainly due to the fact that there was hardly enough room to walk along the length of the bar or between the small round tables scattered throughout the enclosed area.

At those tables, grim-faced men did everything from play cards to arm wrestle. And among those men, there were even a fair amount of women. In fact, the more Clint looked around the place, the more he had to bump up his original estimate of how many people were crammed into the saloon.

Either more were pouring in all the time, or everyone in there was exceptionally talented at filling the space like a nest of vipers slithering in a massive knot of their own kind. Wanting to keep up his appearance as one of those vipers, Clint spotted half an empty spot at the bar and elbowed his way into it. The men on either side of him tossed out a few choice profanities, but still allowed him to stand at the stack of crates without challenge.

The bartender was a stocky man in his late thirties wearing clothes that should have been put out to pasture years ago. There wasn't one square inch of his shirt or pants that weren't stained, torn or both. When he walked up to Clint's spot holding a dirty tin cup, his head snapped back as though he'd been jabbed on the nose.

"You're new here," the bartender said as if that was a revelation.

Clint nodded. "Yeah. Does that mean I can't have a drink?"

Shaking the surprise off his face, the bartender replied, "Didn't mean to offend you, but we hardly ever see an unfamiliar face around here." He looked around as though he expected trouble and when he didn't find any, he shrugged and went on. "What'll it be?"

"There anything in those kegs over there?"

"Sure. I brew it myself," the barkeep replied proudly. "Most of these sons of bitches don't know what's good for 'em and drink nothin' but whiskey."

"Well, I'll try some of that beer. I just better not regret it."

"You won't, mister, you won't." Heading over to the nearest keg, the barkeep filled the cup with foamy beer and walked back over to where Clint was waiting. "Tell you what. You don't like it and I won't make you pay for it."

Remembering the part he was trying to play, Clint narrowed his eyes and said, "If I don't like it, you couldn't make me pay if you tried." The threat wasn't so much in the words, but in the snarling tone in which they were spoken.

The bartender obviously picked up on the subtle threat and raised both hands after setting down the cup. "Like I said, just try it for yerself and you won't be sorry."

Clint was tentative at first, but took a sip of the beer. The smell of it reached his nose before any of the liquid touched his lips. It was bitter and slightly acidic, settling straight into the back of his throat. His first sip was small and just enough to get some of the liquid onto his tongue.

All the while, the bartender watched as though he was on trial for his life. The closer the cup got to Clint's mouth, the stronger his anticipation became.

Once the initial bitterness faded, Clint raised his eyebrows and looked down at the cup in his hand. From there, he nodded and took a bigger sip. This time, all he got was a rich, slightly wooden taste which somehow managed to work in favor of the beer in question.

"Well?" the barkeep asked. "What's the verdict?"

"As much as I'd like to get a free drink out of you, my conscience wouldn't allow it." Seeing the confusion on the other man's face, Clint added, "This is some of the best damn beer I've had in a while!"

That dispelled all the tension on the barkeep's face and caused him to rock back proudly on his heels while beaming a smile to the rest of the saloon. "I told you so! You hear that, you sons of bitches?" he said to the rest of the people in the place, none of whom were actually listening to him. "I've been telling you all for all this time that you didn't know what you were missing!"

He did get a few replies from the others, but all of them were requests for him to shut his hole rather than for a cup of his beer. Still, the barkeep didn't let that dampen his spirits as he collected the money Clint put onto the bar for his beer. "Tell you what. The next one's on me, stranger. Welcome to Dead End Pass."

Clint tipped his cup to the enthusiastic barkeep and turned around to lean against the bar. He was just on time to set his eyes upon a tall, shapely brunette walking toward him, staring him down like he was on a menu.

Now that, he thought, *is what I call a welcome wagon.*

TWENTY-SIX

She strode through the crowd as though there wasn't anyone at all standing between herself and Clint. Her light brown eyes locked onto him and when she saw that he'd noticed her, a seductive smile crept onto her full, luscious lips.

Hair that was darker than black cascaded over her shoulders, spilling down across the front of a dress made out of worn, thick cotton. The dress looked like it had been conservative at one time, but had since been modified by well-placed rips and tears. One such tear ran down the left side, exposing the smooth, creamy skin of her leg as she walked.

To say he was impressed with her body wouldn't have come close to what Clint was truly feeling. He couldn't take his eyes off her if he wanted to, which was perfect because he sure as hell didn't want to. Instead, he watched her come forward, stalking like a cat intent upon its prey.

"Hello there," she said, extending her hand palm down. "I don't think I've had the pleasure."

Clint took her hand and kissed it. The move wasn't what he would have chosen to maintain his abrasive disguise, but he'd simply acted on reflex. Judging by the look in her eyes, the brunette didn't mind his slip one bit.

"I'm Matt Hendershott," Clint said.

"Susan Chambers. You're new here."

"I sure am. Just got here a couple minutes ago. I was beginning to think my horse was the prettiest thing in this place. It's nice to be proven wrong."

Nodding as though Clint had made it past some kind of marker in her head, she stepped forward until she was pressed against Clint's chest. Although she only stayed there for a second, the moment was good enough to stretch out in Clint's mind.

Her breasts were large and firm, wrapped tightly in the dress that had also been ripped down the front so the neckline plunged halfway down her cleavage. The muscles under her skin could be felt against Clint's body. While she was soft to a degree, there was also a hardness about her which somehow took nothing away from her femininity.

When she stepped to one side and shoved into a spot next to Clint, there was a sudden hardness to him as well.

"So did Sonny bring you here?" she asked.

"No. Actually, it was Jeremiah."

"Good. The only ones Sonny brings are here to enjoy their last moments on this earth."

"Is that a fact? Well, then, I guess I'm lucky."

She smiled at that and looked him up and down, allowing her eyes to linger on his chest and then below his belt. "You might be luckier than you think. So far, you're doing pretty well."

"How long have you lived here?"

"Not long. I do work for Sonny every now and then, so I get a place to live here. It beats the hell out of some dry little town where I'd be expected to go to church and sit in a sewing circle or some such nonsense."

"I'll drink to that," Clint replied, raising his glass. "And so will you." Turning toward the barkeep, he said, "Fix her up with whatever she wants."

Susan nodded toward the man behind the bar and waited for him to bring her a tin cup filled halfway with red wine. The bottle had been tucked away between the beer kegs and that's right where it went once her drink had been poured.

"That's very generous of you, Matt. Especially considering that there's no charge for anything in here anyhow."

"Really?" Clint turned to glare at the barkeep.

"Sure. Everything in here's stolen except for that coyote piss in those kegs."

Although the man tried to slink away as soon as he heard Susan say that, the bartender wasn't quick enough to escape. Suddenly brimming with humor, he took Clint's money from his pocket and handed it over. "I gladly accept donations, though. Besides, it was just a little joke for the newcomer."

This time, when Clint glared back at the bartender, he didn't have to think about staying in character to get it right. There was more than enough menace in his eyes to cause the barkeep to back away and find something else to do at another section of the bar.

When he looked back to Susan, the intensity in his eyes was still there but was filled with a different emotion entirely. "Guess I can't really expect a fair deal from a town full of robbers, huh?"

Susan smiled and took a sip of her wine. "I guess not." So far, she hadn't taken her eyes off of him from the moment Clint had turned around. Her gaze was many things at once: enticing, observant, sharp and even piercing. There was an intelligence in her features that spoke volumes for the type of person she truly was.

"Speaking of robbers," she said. "Why would Jeremiah want to bring you all the way to his private little town?"

"I guess he saw some potential in me."

She nodded at that. "I can understand that. But it usually takes more than potential to catch his eye. There's plenty of good robbers out there who wind up dead, shot by Sonny or Jeremiah himself. What did you do to set yourself apart from them?"

"I held up a wagon, wounded the driver and killed both guards," Clint replied without so much as a moment's hesitation.

"That'll set you apart, all right. Do you do things like that a lot, or was this a special occasion?"

"When I know what I want," Clint said, moving forward until he was close enough to reach out and run his hand over Susan's hip, "I do whatever it takes to get it."

She shifted her hips beneath his touch, making a noise in the back of her throat that was something close to a purr. Taking a breath deep enough to push her breasts against the confines of her dress, she tossed her hair back over one shoulder. "And you think everything you want you can just take?"

"I knew that the moment I saw you sizing me up from the other side of this room."

"You're a very observant man, Matt. Come on," she said, taking him by the hand and leading him toward the door. "I want to show you some of the sights."

TWENTY-SEVEN

The last thing Clint had in mind when starting this task was sight-seeing. Of course, when he'd started, he had no way of knowing that one of those sights would be the inside of a small cabin that was mostly filled by a large bed and a single chest of drawers. While not too impressive on its own, that cabin did have its merits—namely, the stunning sight of Susan Chambers kneeling on that bed and peeling her dress away from her body so slow that Clint thought he would burst just by watching her.

Susan had taken Clint from the bar and across the camp in a straight line. The closer she got to her cabin on the outskirts of the camp, the faster her steps became until she was practically running for her own front door. Once she pulled him inside, she slammed the door shut, locked it and kissed Clint with enough passion to take the breath straight from his lungs.

Her lips burned against his mouth and her tongue flicked between his lips. She kissed him even as she backed toward her bed, her hands never leaving his body as she felt the muscles of his shoulders and arms. Without missing a step, she crawled back onto her bed and pressed the palms of her hands flat against Clint's chest.

Her full, light red lips curled into a smile that didn't even attempt to hide how much she wanted him. Susan moved onto the middle of her bed and started slowing removing her dress from her body. First, she slid her fingers down along the neckline, pulling apart the buttons as she came to them. From there, she eased the top down to expose her full, rounded breasts.

As much as he savored every instant of watching Susan undress, Clint couldn't help but wonder if he was dreaming. He didn't seriously think that he was asleep somewhere, but that was also what he'd thought when he'd been making love to Layla several nights ago.

Susan slid the dress farther down, baring a taut stomach and tight, rounded hips. She hooked her thumbs into the sides of her panties and slid them off as well in one, smooth motion. The thatch of hair between her legs was the same dark black as the hair that flowed down around her head and shoulders.

When she removed the dress completely, she let her fingers stay between her legs so she could run them along the moist lips of her pussy. Once her fingertip made it to the sensitive nub of her clitoris, she arched her back and let out a low, shuddering moan.

At that moment, watching Susan pleasure herself and feeling the intense longing growing inside of him, Clint didn't give a damn if he was dreaming or not. Either way, he just wanted to enjoy the moment and get his hands on any part of Susan's soft, naked body.

Clint pulled some of his own clothes off as he moved toward her bed. The cabin was so small that it only took him a few steps to get there, but still he had almost stripped completely by the time he arrived. Susan kept one hand between her legs and used the other to pull Clint forward, her eyes widening when he reached out to embrace her around the waist.

His cock was rigid when she reached down to take hold

of it. Feeling its length within her grasp, Susan let out a deep breath and stroked him at a strong, slow pace. Clint was kneeling on the bed also, his arms wrapped around her to keep her close.

One hand wandered down her back to cup her firm buttocks. When he pulled her closer, she moved her knees apart so she could feel his erect penis slide between her thighs. She put both her hands upon him then, arching her back and grinding against his rigid cock as she got wetter against him.

Taking hold of Clint by the shoulders, Susan pulled her head forward and looked him directly in the eyes. She moved her hips until she felt the tip of his penis rub against the moist lips between her legs. One gentle push was all it took for Clint to enter her and he slid all the way inside while pulling her closer with both hands.

With both of them kneeling and facing each other, Clint and Susan had to lean back slightly for him to enter her all the way. They gripped each other's hands tightly and leaned back even more as he pumped his cock in and out of her.

Susan pulled herself upright and looked at him with wide, excited eyes. She then scooted back and pushed him down with such force that both of Clint's shoulders hit the mattress with a thump. Before he knew which end of the bed his head was at, Clint felt Susan climbing on top of him.

She didn't just mount him, however. She rubbed her wet pussy against his cock, teasing him with her soft dampness while nibbling his chest, neck and ears. Then, she crawled forward, grabbing hold of the post at one corner of the bed.

Clint let his tongue slide over every inch of Susan's body as she moved over the top of him. He'd started at her neck and merely had to lean back to taste her shoul-

ders, breasts, stomach and finally her thighs before she
came to a stop.

Up close, Clint could see the taut muscles in Susan's
legs and thighs as she lowered herself down onto his
mouth. He looked up and saw her looming over him and
looking down like an approving goddess. Her breasts jut-
ted out proudly and her eyes watched him expectantly
until Clint's tongue brushed enticingly over the lips of her
pussy.

"Oh . . . oh, yes," she whispered.

In the confines of the cabin, those soft, breathy words
filled up every bit of space. The bed creaked as Susan
gripped the post even tighter, adding another layer to the
erotic sounds floating throughout the room.

The more Clint flicked his tongue against her sensitive
skin, the quicker Susan's breaths became. Soon, she was
trembling on top of him, grabbing hold of the post with
one hand while sliding her other through her long black
hair and over her breasts.

Clint could feel her reacting to every little move he
made. He played her like an instrument and took his time
licking circles around her clit before finally sliding his
tongue inside of her. He could feel her body tensing at
the brink of an orgasm and when he buried his tongue
inside of her, Susan's pleasure exploded.

Once she'd recovered from the first climax, Susan
eased herself back down along Clint's body until her
pussy was once again brushing against his cock. She got
her feet beneath her and squatted over him, lowering herself down using the muscles in her legs while spreading
herself wide open to accept him inside of her.

She tossed her hair from one side to another as she
rode up and down along the length of his penis. Sometimes she would squat all the way down and he would
push up with his hips so every inch of him was pumping

up into her body. Susan let out deep, heavy breaths that got more passionate every time she took him deep inside of herself.

Clint could feel his own orgasm coming as well and braced himself against the bed for when it finally arrived. He watched Susan riding him, taking in the gentle bounce of her breasts as she moved up and down, watching the sway of her hair as she moaned and writhed in ecstasy.

It felt so good that the possibility of it all being another dream popped into Clint's mind. He reached up and held her hips, which were tight with the strain of her muscles and moist with perspiration. Her nipples were erect under his thumbs as he moved his hands upward.

Suddenly, Susan straightened her back and threw her head back. Wrapped up in the passion of another orgasm, she lowered herself all the way down until she was sitting on Clint's cock and then reached around to slap him playfully on his side.

It wasn't quite a pinch, but at least Clint knew he wasn't dreaming.

TWENTY-EIGHT

Clint stayed in Susan's cabin for the rest of the night. It wasn't until several hours after sundown that they took a long enough rest for him to get a good look at the room itself. Susan was lying on top of her covers, completely naked and basking in the moonlight that came in from between her drawn curtains. Her skin looked especially smooth in the pale light and Clint had to fight his impulses to keep from waking her up and initiating yet another round of lovemaking.

The only thing that stopped him from doing that was when he reminded himself of why he was in this neck of the woods to begin with. He wasn't at Dead End Pass to take in the sights or even wrestle with a gorgeous brunette.

He was there to get to the bottom of a string of murders and robberies. He was there to end Sonny Byrnes's career once and for all. And just recently, he'd learned that he could also take down the infamous Jeremiah Proffit while he was at it.

Outside her window, there was still a constant flow of noise that had been there when he'd arrived and hadn't quieted down all night. It was the noise of several dozen sets of idle hands planning their next trip into the devil's playground. Although the noise of moving feet and whispering voices was slightly less than it had been before, Clint would have preferred things to be more settled outside the cabin before he ventured outside.

Figuring he might never get total quiet in a hidden town full of men used to lurking in shadows, Clint slipped out of bed and got his clothes. He sifted through his belongings and did a quick check of his pockets to make sure everything was still there.

He smirked in the dark when he came across an empty pocket which had been previously stuffed with a small wad of bills. Since most of his money was still sewn into the lining of his belt, Clint didn't bother searching Susan's things just to get back the money he'd set aside for daily expenses.

There were bigger fish to fry and all of them lay outside the cabin's door.

Clint's dented pocket watch was still in its proper place and when he popped it open, he saw that it was a little past three in the morning. Susan was lying in bed, her body still naked and inviting beneath the sheets. Clint figured that she might be faking her own slumber, but he decided to take that chance rather than risk waking her up while checking on her.

Once his clothes and boots were on, Clint opened the door just enough for him to squeeze through and then closed it again behind him. He'd done his best to memorize much of the layout of the little town as he'd gone through it, but his walk to the cabin had been very quick and very distracting to say the least.

Even so, Clint had no problem navigating past the other cabins and pointing himself in the direction he wanted to go. As far as he could tell, nobody had seen him leave the cabin. There were voices nearby and figures in the shadows, but they all seemed too wrapped up in their own business to notice him.

When Clint's mind drifted to how he would handle himself if worse came to worse, his hand drifted to the Colt holstered at his side. Susan had been through his pockets, so just to be safe he took out the modified pistol and flipped open the cylinder.

The smirk that blossomed on Clint's face wasn't from happiness, but from the satisfaction of keeping one step ahead of everyone else. Just as he'd figured, the Colt's cylinder was empty. It was a simple matter of refilling it using the spare shells on his gun belt, but the matter wouldn't have been simple at all if he'd made that discovery when his life depended on it.

Now loaded, the Colt was dropped back into its holster and Clint moved forward through the night.

Instead of trying to stay hidden in the unknown territory, Clint merely did his best to keep out of sight, but walked with his head up and a purpose in his stride. He put himself in the frame of mind that he had things to do, places to be and every right to be there. That was enough to discourage the few others who looked his way. And if someone did seem overly interested in where Clint was going, Clint would simply ignore them.

All of those simple devices were enough to get Clint to the corral without having to explain himself to a soul. The horses were kept away from the main part of the little town anyhow, so there really wasn't much of a reason to stop Clint anyway.

Clint glanced behind him more carefully as he approached the corral, making doubly sure that he wasn't being watched or followed. Being more in the open, he couldn't see anyone close enough to concern himself with or any glares pointed in his direction.

He wasn't about to let his guard down, however. After

jumping over the split rail fence, Clint headed straight over to where Eclipse was tethered and patted the stallion's muzzle. The corral was a far cry from a stall in a good stable, but the men of Dead End Pass weren't stupid. They took care of their animals and each of the horses were provided with plenty of food and fresh water.

But it wasn't the Darley Arabian that Clint was worried about. The reason for his late night visit lay on the other side of the fenced in space and stood like a row of over-sized tombstones in the cold autumnal night.

Clint set his eyes on the wagons he'd spotted earlier and began walking toward them when he heard something that made him freeze in his tracks.

"What's that?" came a voice from not too far away.

Clint couldn't see exactly where the voice was coming from, but he knew the speaker had to be less than ten yards away. More than likely, it was someone on their way to the saloon or one of the tents since those were the closest things to the corral.

"I don't know," came a second voice. "You're the one that stopped like you saw a ghost or somethin'."

"Ghost, my ass. I saw something movin' over by the corral."

"Well, let's go take a look. It's either that or hear you grouse about it the rest of the night."

Clint pulled in a slow, deep breath. His hand closed around the grip of his Colt as he prepared to deal with the approaching visitors.

TWENTY-NINE

Both men had such dirty faces that their skin practically blended in with the night itself. Upon closer inspection, one of the men had skin that was naturally that color anyway, so the dirt only made him blacker. The men's eyes were squinting and they darted to and fro in reaction to every last noise they heard.

Their steps were slow and cautious and both of them had their guns drawn before they stepped foot into the corral.

"I still don't see anything," the black man said. "You're probably just drunk."

The other man stared into the corral as he thumbed back the hammer of his revolver. "I ain't drunk. I saw somethin' moving."

"Yeah, there's plenty of things movin'. Too bad they're all horses."

"I heard something, too. Just shut up and—" He cut himself off as his head cocked to one side. "Over there," he said, pointing to the horses. "See it?"

The black man squinted, his body tensing in reaction to the other man's voice. "See what?"

"There's someone there, I know it."

"So what if there is?"

"If someone's hidin', that means they're up to something. And if they're up to something, we don't need them around here. I'll bet it's some deputy pokin' around or maybe a bounty hunter."

"A bounty hunter?" the black man said, pulling open the corral's gate. "Sonny's offerin' fifty dollars for each bounty hunter's head we bring him."

They each stepped into the corral and became perfectly quiet. Now they were both searching the darkness with equal intensity. The longer they waited, the tighter their fingers squeezed around their triggers. The hammers of both men's guns raised tentatively in preparation for the final drop onto the blasting cap.

Suddenly, there was a jolt of movement from the back of the line of horses. It was a flicker of motion that burst out from the shadows and flew toward both men so quickly that one of them fired a startled shot before he could even take enough time to aim.

All of the horses in the corral reared and let out startled noises at the sudden sound of the shot. All of the horses except for one, that is. And that single horse stayed on all fours even though it shifted anxiously on its feet.

"Jesus Christ!" the black man said once the echo of his partner's shot had receded into the surrounding basin. His voice soon shifted into another sound altogether: laughter. When he got a clear look at the skinny coyote that had run through the horses' legs to cause all the ruckus, that laugh began to shake him from head to toe.

"Goddammit," the first man said, his gun still smoking in his hand. "Goddamn coyote."

After holstering his pistol, the black man ribbed the other one jokingly. "Yeah, but that goddamn coyote scared the shit out of you."

Humiliated, the first man turned on the balls of his feet and stalked out of the corral. "Just shut the hell up and come on before Cletus drinks up all the whiskey again."

Both men walked toward the saloon in relative quiet until the black man could no longer keep himself from saying, "We'd best hurry before we run into another one of those terrible coyo—"

"I said shut up!"

Clint's hand was still on the grip of his Colt as the two men's voices faded away. He waited until their footsteps had gone as well before letting out the breath he'd been holding. His back and knees were starting to cramp even though he'd only been holding his position for a couple of minutes.

His feet were lined up one behind the other with his front toe pointing straight at the back of Eclipse's rear hoof. The hand that wasn't resting upon the Colt was pressed against the stallion's flank, calming him and keeping his from rearing no matter what shots went off or how much the other animals were fretting.

"Good boy," Clint whispered.

Thanks to the Darley Arabian's size and temperament, Clint had been able to crouch and twist himself so that all but the side of one leg was hidden behind his horse's body. What little pieces of him weren't blocked from view were obscured by shadows, which had been enough to keep him from being seen.

Of course, he would have been discovered if those two had stepped into the corral much farther. That problem had been solved with a well thrown pebble against the rear end of a coyote that had been hiding just like Clint.

Now that it was again just him and the horses in the corral, Clint hurried up and took a look at what he'd come to see.

Those wagons were lined up like ducks in a row, making it easier for Clint to glance over them one by one. The first thing he noticed was that each of them sported their fair share of bullet holes and powder burns. That squared away the fact that they'd been taken in the course of a robbery or some other violent exchange.

The next things to catch his attention were letters carved into the wagons on a spot below the driver's seat and a little ways back along the bed. The letters read, MCPIKE SHIPPING and a bit of quick checking told him that those letters had been carved on every last wagon in that corral.

But there was something else that caught Clint's attention besides just the lettering. It was the planks upon which the letters had been carved. There really wasn't anything too special about the lumber itself. It was the same as any other lumber used to build a wagon of that size and cut into planks of a fairly uniform shape.

That was when it finally all fit together inside of Clint's mind.

He'd seen planks like those recently, but not in the shape of a wagon. In fact, he'd seen so many of them that it was no wonder they'd stuck out in Clint's mind.

Slipping away from the wagons and past Eclipse so he could give the stallion one last scratch behind the ears, Clint left the corral and headed toward the main body of the town. As he walked, he looked on either side of him, his eyes darting back and forth in a constant, flicking motion.

He wasn't looking to see if he was being followed. Indeed, he didn't even pay much attention to the faces he passed. What he was looking at was the town itself. More specifically, he was studying the shacks and cabins that made up the pieced together town.

The more he saw, the more he nodded to himself. Once he got to a place that was fairly secluded, Clint stepped up to one of the crooked shacks so he could take a closer look. It took a bit of searching, but Clint eventually found something that made him step back, run his finger along the side of the cabin and shake his head.

"I'll be damned," he whispered to himself.

The space where he ran his finger was where something was carved into the side of the cabin. Actually, the letters were carved into that particular plank. The letters spelled out, MCPIKE SHIPPING.

Not only had Jeremiah Proffit and Sonny Byrnes made off with the wagons in the corral, but they'd stolen enough to tear them apart and use the lumber to build parts of their own little town. Clint knew the robbers had been busy, but this was damn near unbelievable.

THIRTY

Clint took a walk around town, studying the more permanent structures along the way. Sure enough, all of the shacks and even bits of the saloon were made out of planks that were the same size and shape as the ones used to put the wagons together. As if he needed any more proof, Clint also found plenty of bullet holes, powder burns and company names as well.

During his walk through the settlement, Clint counted three other company names carved into some of the lumber used to build the town. Apparently, the robbers were proud of their little innovation because the company names were proudly displayed on the walls of the shacks, usually fairly close to the doors.

The sun was just starting to make its first appearance of the day when Clint made his way back to his tent. Just as he'd figured, anything that was worth more than a nickel had been taken from his saddlebags during the course of the night. Even though there wasn't much left to guard, Clint bundled up the leather bags and set them at the back of the tent. He then laid down and stretched out upon the cold ground so he could set his head upon the bags.

Unlike most other towns, the closer it got to dawn, the quieter this one became. With his eyes almost all the way closed and his hands folded across his belly, Clint listened to the world around him and did his best to relax for a little while.

What he got was a far cry from sleep, but it was restful enough to allow some of the knots in his back and shoulders to loosen. He felt himself drift off even though he never once allowed his eyelids to drop completely shut. He left enough space between them for him to make out the opening of his tent and the occasional movement passing outside of it.

As he drifted off, Clint didn't even realize that his hands had unfolded and one had dropped down to rest upon the modified Colt at his side. The familiar steel felt comforting to him, which was the final straw that allowed him to slip into something close to sleep.

He awoke with a start.

Someone was nearby and even before he figured out who it was or where they were, Clint was sitting up and had the Colt drawn and ready to fire.

Although the face staring in at Clint was smiling, it was anything but friendly. The man's cheeks were sprouting rough stubble and they were covered with pockmarks. His lips were curled back to reveal yellow, cracked teeth. Even at the back of the tent, Clint could smell the rank odor of the other man's breath.

"Hold on there, partner," the other man said. "I jus' came by to wake you. No need to be unfriendly."

Clint fell immediately into character. Part of that was because since he hadn't bathed or shaved in some time, he felt almost as bad as that other man looked.

"Unfriendly?" Clint snarled. "I think I got plenty of reasons to be unfriendly."

The mangy face twisted into an unsure expression and

the smile turned into something that was a lot more cautious. "I don't reckon I know what you're talking about."

Clint's hand flashed upward so quickly that the other man looked amazed when he found himself staring down the barrel of the modified Colt. Holding the pistol in front of him like a deadly promise, Clint sat the rest of the way up and moved closer to the front of the tent.

"Where's my spyglass?" Clint asked.

"Your what?"

"My spyglass. Come to think of it, everything but some scraps of beef jerky and some coffee rounds were taken from my bags. Where are they?"

"You can't expect me to——"

"To what? Die when I pull this trigger? Oh yeah. I expect you to do that soon enough."

Now the other man's eyes became wide as saucers and he started to back out of the tent altogether. He stopped when he saw the disapproving look in Clint's eyes and stopped himself before he could finish reaching for his own sidearm.

"Hold it, now," the dirty man said. "I may recall some others sticking their noses in here, but I don't recall who they were."

"You'd best start recalling. I may not have much in this world, but I sure as hell won't stand by and let some other goddamn dogs take it. You understand me?"

"Yeah, yeah. I understand."

"Whatever happened to honor among thieves, anyway?"

The mangy fellow smirked and shrugged his shoulders. "You was the one that left it lying here, mister."

Clint shook his head and steeled himself as though he was preparing for the Colt's recoil once he pulled its trigger. "Wrong answer."

"I . . . I'll find your stuff for you. All right? Will that do?"

Clint eased up a notch and nodded. "It's a start. Bring back my things soon enough and I might not track you down and shoot you in front of God and all your friends."

Surely threats flowed in Dead End Pass thicker than water or even the air. That was why Clint made sure to put the right edge to his words so they were taken very, very seriously. Judging by the trace of fear in the mangy thief's eyes, Clint had done a fine job.

"I'll do my best."

"Good," Clint said, lowering the Colt without actually holstering it. "Now did you wake me for a reason or did you just pick the wrong man to hassle so early in the morning?"

"Oh, yeah. Sonny wants to talk to you." Jabbing his finger across the way, he added, "He's in that cabin right over there."

"Fine. Now get out of my sight and don't come back until you've got something to hand over to me."

Clint watched as the other man scampered back and finally took off running away from the tent. As much as he hated to admit it, putting the fear of God into that worm didn't feel half bad. Even walking in a snake's skin had the occasional advantage.

THIRTY-ONE

Clint was surprised to find that Sonny Byrnes didn't live in one of the larger cabins. Although he did have one of the sturdier-looking ones, Clint guessed that Susan's cabin was probably a bit bigger than the one used by the man who seemed to be second-in-command of the entire gang.

When he arrived at the cabin, Clint knocked once. The door was pulled open almost immediately to reveal Sonny himself standing on the other side. He wore jeans, a shirt that hung loosely at the waist and he stood in bare feet. Despite his tussled appearance, the look on his face was all business and he waved Clint inside with a curt sideways nod.

"Sit down," Sonny said. "What did you say your name was?"

"Matt Hendershott."

"Yeah. Right. Sit down, Matt."

The cabin consisted of one room. At the far end of the room was a cot just big enough for a man of Sonny's size. Next to the cot was a large battered chest that looked as though it might have been taken from one of the robber's successful jobs. There were bands of dented iron around the chest and a large lock holding it shut. Powder burns

stained the sides and front, which led Clint to believe that
it had probably been blasted open at least once.

The front half of the cabin was taken up by another
large chest which had no lock, a small round dinner table
and two battered wooden chairs that looked as if they'd
been crafted from partially used firewood. Sonny lowered
himself onto one of those chairs, so Clint sat down onto
the other.

"How long you been in this line of work?" Sonny
asked.

"All my life, more or less. I stole as soon as I could
walk."

"What about killing? How long've you been doing
that?"

"Only when it's necessary," Clint replied. "That kind
of thing isn't good for business."

Sonny's eyes were cold as ice and he only moved when
he absolutely had to. Apart from the rising and falling of
his chest and the occasional blink, he was completely mo-
tionless. "Sometimes killing is the business. I saw how
you took out them two wagon drivers the other day, so
don't you sit there and tell me you never was a paid assassin. Only professional killers pull the trigger like that."

Clint knew he was playing a part just as he knew he
hadn't killed those two guards. But there was something
in the way Sonny talked to him that hit a nerve. Although
he never would consider himself a murderer, Clint had
buried more than his share of men. Every one of them
had been necessary, but that didn't take away from the
fact that there were a whole lot of them.

Clint had always told other men of the gun to watch
themselves before pulling the trigger became too easy.
And in the back of his mind, he'd carried that same concern for himself. Being confronted about it even under
these circumstances had its impact, which Clint didn't
even try to hide.

"I do what I have to in order to live to see the next day," Clint finally said. "Just like you or any other man who's chosen to live outside the law. I'm not an assassin and I never will be. Shooting those men yesterday was necessary, but I didn't take any money for it. I'm not a murderer. Am I a killer? You're damn right I am and every man I killed I'd kill again if need be. Is that what you brought me in here to ask?"

Without meaning to, Clint's tone had taken on an aggressive edge. Although Sonny didn't back away from the aggression in Clint's voice, he didn't just shake it off right away either. Clint could see the shift in Sonny's eyes that would have gone unnoticed to anyone who didn't know exactly what to look for.

"You don't have to explain to me the difference between murderer and an assassin," Sonny said, his mouth forming the words while the rest of his face remained etched in stone. "I've been both and more in my time and know the difference well enough. What I need to know is whether you can kill on command."

"I did just fine yesterday."

"Yeah, but was that because you knew you were dead if you didn't put a bullet through them two men."

Clint didn't answer that because Sonny seemed to have just put the question out there for himself to ponder. As he studied Clint's every move and word, Sonny took it all in and didn't miss a thing. "Why do you want to be a part of this gang?"

"Because I hear it's the best," Clint answered. "Simple as that."

"And what do you want in return?"

"Just my fair share."

"Seems to me like you may be worth more than that."

Now, that was something Clint hadn't been expecting.

"That surprise you?" Sonny asked, picking up immediately on the change in Clint's eyes.

"Frankly, yes. I just hoped to go in with you and Mister Proffit. I didn't expect anything more than that."

"Well, we have plenty of thieves and gun hands along with us, but not a lot of real dangerous men. I saw enough of the way you took on that wagon, even though we were too far out to do much about it. And I watched how you handled them other two we sent you to get rid of.

"That kid that we sent to keep watch on you, Dell, has been with us for a bit and he never would've taken out two men like you did. It was quick and clean, Matt. You done a good job."

Clint nodded, unable to look more appreciative than that. It didn't matter what his character was or whether or not those guards were still alive. He simply couldn't look happy about being a killer.

"Go talk to Jeremiah," Sonny said after a few quiet moments. "And get some sleep tonight. Susan is a fine piece of tail, but you'll need your strength."

As Clint got up and headed out of the cabin, he got the distinct impression that he'd passed some kind of test. The meeting had lasted only a few minutes, but Sonny seemed to have drawn some conclusion in his own mind that had tipped the scales.

Despite all his skill at reading people, Clint still couldn't say if the balance had been swung in his favor or not. That put an icy knot in the bottom of Clint's stomach as he left, making him wonder if he might still get shot in the back before leaving that cabin.

THIRTY-TWO

That was the longest five feet that Clint had ever walked.

Since Clint couldn't say for sure if he was truly in the robber's good favors, every muscle in his body tensed as he left the cabin. He felt his hand itching to draw the Colt just to be on the safe side.

But the shot he'd been anticipating never came. When the door shut behind him, Clint felt cool relief flow over him like a spray of ocean mist. Outside, there were plenty of unfamiliar faces lingering about. They watched Clint leave the cabin as if even they didn't know what was going to happen.

Clint stared down each of those faces in turn and walked up to the closest one. "Where's Mr. Proffit's cabin?" he asked.

The other man nodded toward the structure that would have been Clint's first guess on the location of the gang's leader. It wasn't just the biggest cabin of the lot, but it was also the nicest. In fact, it was the only cabin that had a roof which had any chance of keeping the rain out when a storm rolled through.

Clint headed straight for that cabin and found the door open when he got there. Knocking on the frame, Clint eased the door open and looked inside. "Mr. Proffit? You here?"

Clint could see at least three rooms inside the cabin. One of those was straight back from the door and that was the one that Jeremiah Proffit looked out from in response to Clint's voice.

"There you are, Matt. You won over Sonny's approval I see."

"Did I?" Clint said as he walked inside. "I guess word travels faster than I do."

Walking up to meet Clint with a strong handshake, Proffit said, "I didn't need to get anybody's word for it. The fact that you're here at all tells me that Sonny found something to like about you."

"Would he have just sent me away if he didn't?"

"No. He would have killed you."

Those words hung in the air between them like a cold fog. Suddenly, Proffit snapped out of his serious expression and broke into a wide, welcoming smile. "But that's neither here nor there. You're alive and talking to me now, which is all that matters. Care to sit down?"

"No, thanks. I'd rather stand."

"Funny, but you're not the only man to feel that way after coming to see me after talking to my partner. Believe me, the hard part of your conversations today are over. I want to talk to you about business."

"What kind of business?"

"The kind that'll make us a ton of money. Not just me and Sonny, but everyone in this whole little town of ours stands to ride out of this pass as wealthy folks. I just had one of my men return from a little trip he took for me. I sent him to a telegraph office to check up on some things for me. You know what he found?"

Clint shrugged and shook his head, even though he did have a pretty good idea about what was coming.

"He found out that an office in Green Leaf was broken

into and looted. You know anything about that, Matt?"

"I may have heard some things."

Smiling, Proffit said, "I'll just bet you do. Some things were stolen from that office that might just give a man an idea of where a certain company's next couple of shipments may be headed. Is this sounding a little more familiar now?"

Although Clint maintained his silence, he did so respectfully. He didn't give the other man any smug looks or nasty stares. One thing he knew about thieves and killers was that they took issues of respect very seriously.

"All right then," Proffit said as he stepped up nose to nose with Clint. "Let's cut the bullshit, shall we? Either you were the one that broke into that office or you're working with the man who did the job. Either that, or it was a whole lot of dumb luck that put you onto that shipment, since we both know those shipping schedules are kept locked up tighter than a debutante's pussy."

This was something that Clint most certainly did not know. Although he knew that the schedules were kept under lock and key simply because he'd broken that lock, he didn't know they were such a secret. Most shipping companies didn't advertise their routes, but they usually weren't guarded secrets either.

With all this in mind, he still kept his face neutral as his brain worked feverishly to maneuver around this new information. He knew he needed to work fast, since Proffit didn't look like he wanted to be kept waiting for an answer.

"All right," Clint said. "So maybe I did manage to get my hands on some information. Does that make it any less valuable?"

"No, but it might make it more dangerous. How'd you know I wouldn't just kill you to get those schedules and be done with it?"

"I didn't. But I also didn't think you'd be quick to get

rid of the man who got them when he's willing to come to work for you."

"I've heard that much already. Tell me something else before I lose interest."

"I can be a bigger help to you than just another gun hand."

Proffit's eyes narrowed and he stepped back a couple of paces. Although he hadn't taken his eyes off of Clint since he'd walked through the door, the gang leader now looked at him as though he was trying to get a look at Clint's very core.

"And what are these big notions of yours?" Proffit asked. "You have a bank in mind for us to hit or some nonsense like that?"

"Not quite. My thought was to take Albert Conroy for all he's worth instead of whatever pittance he's been paying you to unleash your gang in the direction he wants."

That caused Proffit to blink once as though he'd been surprised by a flash of light. "Suddenly, Mr. Hendershott, I'm very glad I didn't kill you."

THIRTY-THREE

Clint knew this was a high-stakes game, and in high-stakes games, it was necessary to take the occasional big risk. After all, that was why they called it gambling and not investing.

Saying what he'd just said to Jeremiah Proffit had been a huge gamble. The stakes involved were no less than Clint's life as well as the lives of how ever many other men would be killed by Proffit's gang over the next several jobs.

The name of Albert Conroy had been in the back of Clint's mind because that was the name of Ken McPike's biggest competitor. It seemed that a gang of robbers would hit whatever wagons they could find that were carrying enough to make it worth their trouble. To hit shipments of lumber and building supplies just didn't make sense.

It didn't make sense, that is, unless they were being paid by someone else to hit those shipments. Clint only had to ask around a bit in Green Leaf and flip through a few of the papers he'd found in McPike's office to know that the one man that would pay to have McPike's wagons hit was Albert Conroy.

Clint had had plenty of time to make those connections when preparing to get to the bottom of the gang itself. He'd had enough experience in dealing with businessmen to know that you didn't get anywhere by trying to move on their ground using their rules. Doing so would make swimming through quicksand seem easy by comparison.

That was why he'd gone straight to the source of the violence and worked toward the source of the payment later. Well, Clint was looking at the source of the violence at that very moment when he looked into the eyes of Jeremiah Proffit.

The tricky part now would be to talk his way out of it while keeping his disguise and himself from being shot full of holes.

"How'd you know we were taking money from Conroy?" Proffit asked.

Clint shrugged and told him the absolute truth. "I didn't. It just made sense since McPike's wagons were your favorite target."

"You see a lot, don't you?"

"Yep. What I haven't seen is why shipments of nothing much at all would be hit by a gang like you." Clint leaned in a little and lowered his voice to a conspiratorial whisper even though there was no one else in sight. "I've been dying to ask you. What's really in those wagons? There's got to be something in there besides just nails and boards."

"Take a look around you," Proffit said, extending both arms to encompass the entire cabin. "You want to know what was in those wagons, just look here or look outside."

"You paid for this whole place with what was in there?"

"No. I had it built and I used the nails and boards that we took from all those wagons. Granted, there wasn't quite enough wood to build everything, so we had to tear apart some of the wagons themselves to supply us with the lumber we needed."

"So that was all just building supplies you stole?" Clint asked.

"What was in them wagons didn't matter. Well, not to us anyway. What matters is that we have those supplies and McPike's customers don't." Proffit pulled up a nearby chair from one of the many that were scattered about the room.

Unlike Sonny's cabin, this one was furnished enough to keep an entire family comfortable. The chair that Proffit sat down in was well padded and appeared to have some gold threads woven into the cushion as well. Clint naturally drifted toward one of the more modest chairs and took a load off his feet.

"How'd you hear about what I was doing?" Proffit asked.

"Read about it in a newspaper. I heard that wagons were getting robbed and that Sonny Byrnes was supposed to be one of the men doing the robbing."

"And that's exactly what I wanted people to hear. That's why we let one man go, injured of course, so he could tell folks about what happened."

"You want those men to spread the word?"

"No," Proffit corrected. "I want them to spread their fear. This is all an idea I had some time ago when me and some of my men were setting up to rob a payroll from a stagecoach in New Mexico."

As he spoke to Clint, Proffit's mannerisms became noticeably more relaxed. In fact, he even seemed to be talking to Clint more as an equal than as any kind of threat or even a hired gun. On the contrary, Proffit even seemed friendly now that he had someone to talk to who could appreciate what he'd done.

"Needless to say," Proffit continued, "that payroll had more men guarding it than an army division. Sitting there, waiting for that stage to ride by, waiting to throw myself at all those sharpshooters and shotguns, I wished for the easier days of robbing anything I could get my hands on. You know what I mean. Well, what was your first job that worked out?"

Clint thought for a moment and then smiled as if re-calling a childhood friend. He started shaking his head and looked away from Proffit's anxious eyes.

"Come on," the gang leader insisted. "Let's hear it."

"When I was thirteen, I stuck up this place where I used to live in a little town you probably never heard of in Mississippi. My friend and I just got our hands on our first guns and we were aching to use them, so we screwed up our courage and headed into this store where we al-ways used to buy sticks of candy and sarsaparilla.

"We both thought we were some real bad men and when I stuck my gun in the old man's face who owned the store, I thought I was worse than Jesse James himself. We were both too stupid to do much thinking and all we got out of it was about two dollars and a whole lot of candy. Not to mention that my friend shot me in the foot on our way out."

Proffit started laughing so hard that he had to take a few deep breaths to steady himself. Even Clint had to laugh, despite the fact that he'd borrowed the story from a man he'd spoken to in a jail cell. That, however, was another matter altogether.

Once he was done laughing, Proffit said, "There now. You know what I'm talking about. That store was easy and even fun to rob. Myself, I used to terrorize snake oil salesmen when I was young. My friends and I would shoot up them wagons and get drunk on whatever tonic he was selling.

"The point I'm trying to make is that it was easy! It just didn't pay much. So when I was sitting there ready to rob this payroll and thinking about easier times, I

started to wonder how I could make money out of doing
jobs that wouldn't be such a risk to life and limb. The
answer I came up with was beautiful in its simplicity."
Proffit leaned forward with his elbows on his knees, talking to Clint like a general looking over a map of the
enemy's defenses.

"Businessmen," he said simply. "They're always looking for ways to hurt their competition. Hell, I'd bet they'd
love to kill their competitors if they had the balls to pick
up a gun."

"So you hired yourself out to businessmen to take on
their competition?"

"Not quite," Proffit said, his face beaming with pride.
"I hired my services to them to put them at the top of
their food chain. Killing the head of another company
would be like killing me. You do that, and the next guy
in line moves in to take my place. What I do besides
inflict damage is make the target a pariah in their own
circles. Their entire business dries up, forcing all their
customers to come flocking to whoever has the brains to
hire me."

"So let me get this straight," Clint said. "You robbed
all those wagons just to interrupt shipping schedules?"

Proffit nodded.

"And you let one man escape from each shipment so
they could talk about what happened to anyone who
asked."

Once again, Proffit nodded. "According to my sources,
McPike's earnings have started dropping since my first
attack on his shipments. Since then, they've been falling
like a rock was tied to them."

As the whole picture became clearer in Clint's mind,
he talked it out to the man who'd drawn it. "Someone just
wanting to ship a load of wood and nails won't want to
go through the extra trouble and expense of hiring more
guards. It'd be easier just to switch to another company

that wasn't being targeted by a gang of robbers."

"You're a smart man, Mr. Hendershott. I'm glad you made it this far. I could use a thinking man like yourself to take this scheme of mine to the next level."

Clint didn't like the sound of that one bit. But since he was still entrenched in the character of Matt Hendershott, he put an expression on his face to reflect the exact opposite of what was going on inside him. "There's more?" Clint asked with an eager smile.

"Oh, there's plenty more. Let's just say that I'll be moving up the food chain myself and everyone who's with me will be along for the ride. Everyone who stands against me will be trampled underfoot."

Clint was finding it very difficult to maintain his smile since things seemed to be getting worse by the second.

THIRTY-FOUR

Clint was dismissed from Proffit's cabin very soon after that. Not wanting to say much more about what he had planned, Proffit shared a shot of whiskey with Clint as a way to welcome Matt Hendershott along for the ride of what was to be Proffit's crowning achievement. With the burn of alcohol still running through his system, Clint was asked to leave and encouraged to save his strength for the ride to come.

Details weren't given about when they were planning to head out or what their destination might be, but Clint was assured that he would have plenty to do once the time came. Clint did his best to look pleased at passing his interview with Proffit and left the cabin as soon as he was told to do so. In the back of his mind, however, he'd already decided on another course of action altogether.

He wasn't ten feet away from the cabin's door when he saw a familiar figure headed his way. Clint recognized the intense glare and purposeful stride of Sonny Byrnes the moment the other man came into his line of sight. It didn't take an expert in human nature to know that Sonny was in no mood for anything close to small talk, so Clint stepped to one side and let him pass.

The rest of the day was spent with Clint biding his time and trying to get a feel for the general mood of the town. Much like a camp of soldiers on the eve of a battle, morale was going to play a very important role. Clint may not have known exactly what was on the horizon, but it was going to be big. He was certain of that much at least.

Although he hadn't seen anyone come out of the main cabin since Sonny walked in, Clint could feel the change in the general opinion regarding his own standing within the gang. Almost the instant he was through talking to Proffit, the rest of the men in town started treating him more as an equal.

When Clint went back to his tent, a few of his things had even been returned to his saddlebags. Of course, he wasn't about to read too much into that since it could have been the work of the dirty-faced man trying to save his own skin. But when he went to the saloon, Clint started to read a little more into it.

He wasn't getting any challenging stares as he stepped up to the bar. Of course, he wasn't getting any open arms or welcoming smiles either, but it was definitely a step in the right direction. Clint even saw the improvement when he spotted the barkeep smile warmly and walk right up to him.

"Well, well," the barkeep said. "Care for another cup of my special brew? On the house this time, of course."

"Sure." Once the full cup was set in front of him, he took a sip and asked, "Are the walls around here thin, or have I just made a whole lot of friends overnight?"

"Huh? Oh! The boys around here just know about your meeting with Jeremiah and Sonny, that's all."

"Sure, and it went well, but everyone else seemed to know that as soon as I did."

"Well, you walked out of there, didn't you?"

"Yeah," Clint replied.

"If it hadn't gone well at any time, you would have been carried out."

At that moment, Clint knew that he'd been walking in Matt Hendershott's shoes long enough for them to truly fit him. He was no stranger to having others out to kill him, but this time he merely shrugged and took another sip of beer.

He drank a few more beers over the next several hours and was even asked to join a poker game that was started at one of the little round tables in the back of the place. The stakes were low, but he had to admit the other players had some amusing stories to tell. Although definitely boosted by no small amount of lies, each tale was taller than the one before it and made for a good night's entertainment.

By the time late afternoon turned into night, Clint was still at the same table. He felt a pair of soft hands slide onto his shoulders from behind and immediately recognized the scent of Susan's skin as she sidled up and put her lips next to his ear.

"I hear you made a good impression on Jeremiah," she said.

Clint turned to look at her and saw she was wearing a dress similar to the one from the other night, but with cuts in the material that left even less to the imagination. "I guess so. I'm alive."

Sliding her hands under his shirt and down his chest, she closed her teeth over Clint's earlobe and flicked her tongue against his skin. "Well, I feel like celebrating."

When he got up, it was to a round of hearty applause from all the other men at the table. "Cash me out, fellas," Clint said to the other players. "Looks like I'm wanted elsewhere."

THIRTY-FIVE

Susan was on all fours on her bed, thrashing her hair from side to side as Clint pumped in and out of her. Her nails dug into the covers and she clenched her jaw shut to keep from crying out with the full force of the pleasure she was being given.

It wasn't out of some fear of making noise that she held back, but because preventing herself from moaning out loud only made her orgasm that much more intense. Her breasts were shaking with the force of Clint's powerful strokes and she pushed against him to add her own body to his momentum.

Clint grabbed hold of her hips with both hands as he drove his rigid cock between her thighs. Sweat trickled down his chest just as it ran in little drops down the smooth curve of Susan's spine. Her pussy clenched around him and her back arched, which were the first signs of an impending climax.

She had a way of flexing the muscles between her legs and moving her body to bring Clint to orgasm in time to her own. Leaning forward to cup her large, swaying breasts, Clint drove into her one last time before letting her do the rest of the work.

145

It felt like riding a wave which tossed him up into the air and dropped him down again. Clint's stomach clenched and his breath was taken away as he exploded inside of her and Susan let out a final, shuddering gasp. After that, they both collapsed onto the bed in a hot tangle of arms and legs. . . .

It was dark outside her cabin window and Clint didn't want to waste a second of it. As soon as he felt her breathing become deeper and more steady, he slipped out of her bed and back into his clothes. He was still buckling the gun belt around his waist when he quietly stepped through her door and into the waiting night.

With the effects of the last hour or so of intense love-making still crackling beneath his skin, Clint moved from shadow to shadow like a cat darting toward an unsuspecting mouse. His destination was nothing that was about to escape him so easily, however. Instead, it was something that only a blind man could miss.

It was the largest cabin in Dead End Pass that Clint was after and he slipped up to it without attracting more than a passing glance.

Now that he wasn't under the scrutiny of every last killer in the small makeshift town, Clint was able to get up to the cabin with a minimum of fuss. Besides that, the entire camp seemed to be taking the advice both Sonny and Proffit had given him and were getting their rest. He could hear some other sounds as well which told Clint that not all of the men were alone in their beds.

Either way, compared to the previous night, Clint felt as though he had the run of the camp and was prepared to make the best of it.

Once he was at Proffit's cabin, Clint pressed himself against the side of the building and inched his way toward the closest window. There was a faint flicker of light coming from the other side of the glass, so he made sure to keep his own movements slow and stealthy.

Clint peeked through the lower corner of the window and took a look inside. He stifled a curse before it could slip from his lips when he saw that both Proffit and Sonny were still inside. While Proffit was in the seat that he'd occupied when Clint had been there before, Sonny paced around the room like a caged animal. Clint was just barely able to pull himself down quick enough to avoid being seen when Sonny snapped his gaze toward that particular window.

Before he was spotted by one of the few men wandering about the area, Clint stepped away from the cabin and turned sharply away from the window. He kept his eyes on the glow of the cabin's light thrown onto the ground rather than the window himself. That way, when he saw the vague outline of someone standing at that window, Clint wasn't facing in that direction.

Sonny's wandering stare moved over Clint's back like ghostly fingers. Clint could feel that he was being watched as he walked away, but that only lasted for another few seconds before Sonny stepped away from the window and headed back into his conversation.

As much as Clint wanted to listen in on what was going on inside that cabin, the risk was just too great for him to eavesdrop directly. He'd come too far to ruin everything by being overly anxious at the wrong time. Besides, he already had another place in mind for him to go to that might still hold the answers he needed.

And since he knew Sonny was preoccupied at the moment, Clint figured Byrnes's cabin would be ripe for the picking.

THIRTY-SIX

He was almost right.

It only took a matter of seconds for Clint to get to the run-down little cabin that was Sonny Byrnes's home. When he got there, he found one man standing nearby who didn't seem to have anywhere else to go. Watching from a few yards away while pretending to roll a cigarette, Clint saw that the figure lurking in the shadows was indeed pacing a short line back and forth near the cabin rather than heading somewhere else.

That meant the man was a guard and where there were guards, there was always something worth guarding. Although getting into the cabin wasn't going to be as easy as he might have hoped, Clint was glad to see that he was at least on the right track.

Since the town was pretty much an oversized camp, there were no streets or alleyways to speak of. That made it easier for Clint to sneak around the position where he'd spotted the guard and come up behind the other man.

Clint was getting very good at making his steps look casual and at finding things to occupy his hands or eyes whenever he was spotted by someone else. In fact, he flowed seamlessly from staggering as though he'd been drinking to ducking around the back of the cabin the guard was supposed to be watching.

Sneaking up on the guard, Clint changed his tactic at the last moment and tapped the man on the shoulder. "I'm here to take over for you," Clint said in a bored, slightly aggravated tone. "You're supposed to get some rest."

The other man stretched his arms and rolled his head to work a kink out of his neck muscles. "Yeah, yeah. I swear we got our mommas cracking the whip on us lately."

"I hear you," Clint replied. "Where's the other one that's watching this place?"

Spinning around to face Clint, the guard said, "Other one? What other one? Who sent—"

Before the guard could finish his sentence, Clint had already balled up his fist and taken a short upward swing. Using the same speed he would use to draw his gun, Clint put enough force behind his punch to knock the guard out with one blow.

The other man's face still looked suspicious and aggressive even though the light behind his eyes had been snuffed out. He started to fall away from the wall he'd been leaning against, but Clint's other hand snapped out to take hold of the front of his shirt and pull him back into the shadows.

Clint dragged the unconscious guard farther into the darkness. He took a quick look around. Luckily, there wasn't anyone in the immediate area who might have seen the ambush. But there was also nothing around for him to tie up the guard's hands.

On the bright side, at least Clint had found out there was only one guard watching the cabin. Making do with what was on hand, Clint pulled the guard's belt from around his waist and cinched it tightly around the other man's wrists. There was even enough for him to make a crude loop around his ankles as well, making it all the more difficult for him to go anywhere before Clint was ready.

With the guard secured, Clint tossed the man over his shoulders and headed for Byrnes's cabin. It wasn't the easiest way to go, but there were simply too many people wandering around for him to risk leaving the guard where he was. Also, there weren't any good places to stuff the unconscious body without running the same risk of being discovered.

The cabin door was unlocked. That didn't surprise Clint much since being caught in there without permission was probably not a far cry from suicide. Clint stepped inside and closed the door behind him. Only then did he drop the guard onto the floor and head for the very thing that had caught his attention the last time he'd been in that sparsely furnished shack.

The lockbox was right where it had been earlier that day. It still sat against the wall and it was still wrapped in iron strips that looked even stronger now than they had before. Clint didn't have any time to waste looking at the chest, however. He needed to get inside of it as quickly as possible.

To that end, he was glad that he had paid attention to another little trick from the criminal element. He lit a lantern that had been hanging by the door and twisted the knob so only the smallest flame could rise up from the wick. Setting it down to throw some light onto the chest's lock, Clint removed his knife from its sheath and got to work at breaking the lock open.

Although the chest itself looked old and battered and the iron bands wrapped around it were dented and rusty, the lock keeping it shut seemed to be fairly new. When Clint first tried to get it open, all he managed to do was slice his finger when the knife slipped from the lock. He tried again, only this time keeping his eyes closed so he could let his sense of touch take over.

He couldn't see the inner workings of the lock anyhow, so shutting his eyes gave his mind free reign to visualize what was going on inside that steel casing. After what seemed to be an eternity of fumbling with the blade, Clint felt the knife push a tumbler aside and fit into place. One more twist was all it took for a welcome metallic click to fill his ears.

He felt a rush go through his system that must have been what every thief felt after making it to his illicit goal. Clint opened the chest and lifted the lantern so he could get a better look inside. There were stacks of money tied together with strands of twine and several leather pouches that were too heavy to be filled with anything but gold.

But Clint wasn't there for the money. Instead, he dug right past the more common treasure and didn't stop until he came to the bottom of the chest. Any other thief might have considered the stack of papers to be nothing more than lining, but to Clint it made all the risks worthwhile.

He removed the papers and held them closer to the lantern. On the sheets were written shipping schedules and maps of travel routes. But what made him stop was that the routes weren't for McPike Shipping lines. They weren't even for one of Albert Conroy's wagons.

The papers toward the bottom of the stack were intercepted telegraphs detailing personal travel schedules for the heads of both companies who were set to meet with the Governor of Arizona. Not only that, but the ransom notes for all three men had already been written.

THIRTY-SEVEN

The only thing missing from Byrnes's notes had been the exact routes to be taken by the three potential kidnap victims. There was a timeline that detailed everything from luncheons to private meetings. There was even a list of personal requests made by the governor pertaining to diet restrictions and preferences for hotel accommodations.

Clint read through it all with great interest. The one thing that caught his eye in particular was a section of the schedule designated for a full day's travel. That day just happened to be circled and was only a matter of hours away.

Suddenly, Clint's timetable for dealing with Sonny Byrnes and his friends was history. He knew he wanted to act before anyone else was hurt, but he figured he'd have another couple of days to get further entrenched within the gang. As it was, he figured he'd be lucky to earn a spot on the ride that was set to meet up with the businessmen and governor.

To that end, Clint made one last adjustment to try and stack the deck in his favor. He took one of the leather pouches and topped it off with gold borrowed from one of the other pouches until the one in his hand was full to bursting. He took one of the stacks of money as well and then slammed the chest shut.

The lock had been broken in the process of being opened, but that didn't matter much to Clint. In fact, he figured it would even work in his favor. Every second ticked away in Clint's mind as he set about wrapping up his business inside that cabin. When he was done, he scooped up the unconscious guard and headed out the front door.

Clint took the man back to his post, removed the belt restraining his hands and then jogged over to a nearby water trough. Cupping his hands to scoop up some of the cold water, Clint dashed back to the guard and splashed the water across the other man's face.

He was several yards away by the time the guard sputtered and thrashed himself awake again. Stepping out so he could be seen by a group of bandits staggering away from the vicinity of the saloon, Clint looked around and made himself appear just as confused as everyone else that could hear the guard's coughing and cursing.

"What the hell is that?" one of the nearby men asked.

Clint looked around and finally pointed toward the general area where he knew the sounds were coming from. "I think it's coming from over there."

The more the guard came to his senses, the louder he got. Not only had Clint been hoping for that to happen, he'd counted on it.

"Son of a bitch hit me!" the guard shouted as he jerked up to his feet and bolted toward the closest group of people he could see. "I was bushwhacked! Goddammit, where is that bastard?!"

Like everyone else that had been attracted to the noise, Clint moved toward the guard. He made sure to hang back just enough to be sure that he was toward the back of the group that formed around the spectacle.

The guard charged forward, running his eyes over

every face around him. "Where is he? Where is that son of a bitch?"

"Where is who?" one of the nearby robbers asked. "Who're you talking about?"

But the guard didn't seem interested in explaining himself. Instead, he pushed aside anyone who came up to him so he could get a better look at the others standing nearby. With Clint staying deftly out of sight, the guard was staggering around like a man possessed. He didn't stop until he spotted one familiar face that wasn't exactly the one he'd been looking for.

"What the hell is this?" Sonny growled as he pushed through the crowd to face the man in the middle of it. Spotting the guard, Sonny walked right up to him and said, "Don't you have a job to do?"

"Yeah, but someone said they were stepping in for me. I think it was that new fella." Just then, the guard spotted Clint who'd finally allowed himself to be seen. "There!" he shouted, snapping his arm up and out to point directly at Clint. "There he is!"

What the guard didn't notice right away was the heavy bundle that dropped from where it had been tucked under his belt and beneath the tail of his shirt. All the noise came to an abrupt stop when that pouch landed at the guard's feet with a thump.

Sonny had just started to take on some of his guard's aggression when he noticed the pouch fall. Recognizing it immediately, he glared down at it and then slowly turned a murderous gaze back up to the man in front of him.

THIRTY-EIGHT

The guard had no trouble spotting the rage seething just behind his boss's eyes. "I don't know what that is, Sonny. Here, you can take it." He reached down to pick up the bundle, but was stopped by a crack of gunfire that seemed to drop down upon him like thunder from a mountaintop.

"Don't touch that," Sonny commanded. He didn't have to ask twice since the guard pulled his hand back like it was attached to a spring. Everyone but Sonny himself seemed surprised that the shot hadn't done any damage, but punched a hole in the dirt instead.

Sonny retrieved the bundle and weighed it in his hand. "Where'd you get this?" he asked.

The guard was speechless. Instead of words, the only thing that came out of his mouth were incoherent babbles.

Opening the pouch and glancing inside only made Sonny angrier as his initial suspicions were confirmed. "You were supposed to guard my door, not break through it."

The guard didn't know what to say. The confusion on his face would have been comical if not for the grim specter of death which seemed to be floating over his head. That specter's presence was felt by everyone gathered

155

there and its source was the cold, murderous intensity in Sonny Byrnes's eyes.

Sonny stepped forward and slapped his left hand against the guard's torso. He patted the other man down so roughly that the guard was almost knocked off his balance. Sonny came to an abrupt stop when his hand came to rest upon another bundle stuffed underneath the other man's belt at the small of his back.

"What's this?" Sonny asked, pulling out the bundle. He knew the answer as soon as he felt the bundle and held up the stack of money as if he meant to stuff it down the other man's throat. "I asked you a question. What the fuck is this?"

The guard was white as a sheet and stabbed a finger toward Clint. "It was him! I tell ya, he knocked me out and put those things there! Look for yourself," he added, pointing to the dark red knot on his face where Clint had punched him.

Moving only as much as he needed to look back to where the guard was pointing, Sonny said, "This true, Hendershott?"

Without the slightest hesitation, Clint put on an expression of shocked indignation and replied, "What? Hell, no, it isn't true. I just stepped out to stretch my legs when this asshole starts shouting loud enough to raise the dead."

Sonny glanced around to the others gathered around, studying each face in turn.

"Ask anyone here," Clint said. "I've been walking about for the last couple minutes. Hell, go ask Susan. She'll tell you where I been."

Susan answered her door with a blanket wrapped loosely around her. When she saw the size of the crowd outside her cabin, she hastily pulled the blanket tighter about her to cover her obviously naked body. "What's going on out here?" she asked.

At the front of the crowd, Sonny stood glaring at her. "What've you been doing tonight, Susan?"

"That's my business," she replied, her eyes searching the group behind him.

Still taking up most of her field of vision, Sonny said, "You seem to be lookin' for someone."

"Matt Hendershott. Where is he?"

"Was he here tonight?"

"And what if he was? I don't have to answer to you or anyone else in here, Sonny Byrnes, and you know it."

"Just tell me how long he was with you. It's important."

Susan didn't hide her aggravation. In fact, she wore it like the clothes that weren't on her back at the moment. With her eyes set firmly, her hands on her hips and after an exasperated sigh, she told him, "I came to get him a few hours or so ago. We went back here, we crawled all over each other like we was in heat. We fell asleep, I woke up and I just was about to get dressed to look for him. Happy?"

"When did you wake up?"

"About five minutes ago."

Sonny nodded. "Yeah, Susan. Now I'm happy."

"Do you know where Matt is?"

"He's right here." And with that, the robber stepped aside and let Clint walk past him. "You two can go about your business. I've got some matters of my own to settle right now."

Clint walked into Susan's cabin and let her shut the door behind him. Inside, they could hear the crowd moving away and over the noise of all those boots scraping against the dirt, there was the panicked shouting of the man who'd been guarding Sonny's cabin.

"You gotta believe me, Sonny! I would never steal from you!" the guard pleaded. "Please! Listen to me!"

"I already heard more than enough out of you," came Sonny's steely-edged voice.

After that, even with his ear pressed against the door, Clint couldn't hear anything.

He couldn't hear anything, that is, until there was a single shot that rang through the night as well as Clint's ears so loudly that it might as well have been shot from a cannon.

After the echo of that shot dissipated, the entire basin seemed to let out a breath that it had been holding and the noise level went back to normal.

"What was that all about?" Susan asked as she came up behind Clint.

"Believe it or not, you just saved my life."

THIRTY-NINE

It was early the next morning when every last soul in Dead End Pass was stirred awake. The call rolled throughout the little town like a clap of thunder, starting with the pounding of an insistent hand against the side of a dinner bell. From there, the summons was picked up by others in many different ways, spreading until no one in the basin could possibly be asleep.

Clint was one of the few in the area who didn't need the wake-up call. His eyes may have closed every now and then throughout the night, but there was no way on earth he could get himself back to sleep. Once he'd been shut away in Susan's cabin, Clint had wiled away the hours with her while trying to look as though he didn't have a care in the world.

The fact of the matter was that couldn't have been farther from the truth.

The only time his mind hadn't been racing with one thing or another was when Clint's entire body was kept busy by Susan herself. Even then, he was far from completely distracted. With all that he'd learned the last time he'd ventured out from Susan's bed, Clint had enough to occupy his mind for several lifetimes.

Unfortunately, there wasn't a lot he could do about it until the gang leaders decided to make their next move. Clint had already come close enough to being discovered and called out in front of the entire town. Doing so again would have been akin to signing his own death warrant.

When the knock came upon the cabin door, Clint was already up and mostly dressed. Susan had been stirring as well, but she was more concerned with holding a pillow over her ears to buy a few more moments of peace and quiet. When her leg slipped out and didn't brush against Clint's side, Susan finally tossed the pillow and sat up to take a look for herself.

"What's all the ruckus?" she asked in a voice slurred by fatigue.

Clint was just buckling his gun belt when he told her, "Just sit back and pull those blankets up. You gave everyone enough of a show last night." With that said, Clint went over and pulled open the front door.

Standing outside, wearing a wide, excited smile, was none other than Jeremiah Proffit himself.

"I have good news for you, Matt," Proffit said. "We need all our best men along for this next job and that means you're coming with us. You up for a ride?"

"Yeah, sure," Clint said. "I was hoping that none of that nonsense from last night would make you think less of me."

Proffit waved that off like an insect buzzing around his head. "You ask me, that asshole's probably been stealing from Sonny for months. The only reason he kept getting that job was because he made a few people disappear that had been stealing from Sonny before. After the bloodbath he caused in Prescott, I wanted that guy out of my sight anyway."

Suddenly, Clint didn't feel so bad anymore about how things had turned out for the man he'd set up the other night. He recalled a bank robbery in Prescott involving

Sonny Byrnes that had resulted in the death of three deputies who were guarding the vault. It seemed only fitting that the killer would die acting as a guard himself.

"Don't wait up for this one tonight, Susan," Proffit said to the woman standing behind Clint. "We might be gone for a while, so keep that thing warm for him until he gets back."

"That's a real sweet thought, Jeremiah," Susan said.

Proffit then left and Clint turned around to face Susan, who gave him a kiss on the lips. "Dream about me while you're gone and when you get back, we'll see about making them dreams come true," she whispered.

There was a part of Clint that wanted to do his job and come back to collect on that promise. It was the same part that grew harder as Susan reached down to stroke him while they kissed.

The cold air outside hit Clint in the face like a wet slap. After the heat that had been flooding through his body only seconds ago, the cold did him a world of good.

Proffit wasn't the only one waiting for him outside the cabin. Sonny Byrnes and one other familiar face was outside as well, watching Clint intently as he pulled in a deep breath of morning air. The other face belonged to the kid who'd overseen Clint's shooting of the two wagon guards when he and Proffit had first crossed paths.

"Morning, Dell," Clint said with a tip of his hat.

The kid returned the sentiment with an offhand wave. Apparently, he was still nervous being around someone he thought to be a cold-blooded killer. That only made Clint wonder who Dell thought the rest of the men riding with him were.

Sonny Byrnes looked the same as ever. Colder than a winter's snow. Stonier than the side of a mountain.

The entire town was alive with noise and movement. On every side, there were sounds of people and horses roaming about as well as voices shouting orders from one side to another. One set of hoofbeats were drawing steadily closer and just as Clint turned to look and see if he had to jump out of the way, he heard Proffit's chipper voice behind him.

"I took the liberty of gathering your things and saddling up your horse," he told Clint. "Here he comes now. What a fine animal. Darley Arabian, isn't he? I don't suppose you'd be willing to part with him?"

"Not on your life," Clint said as he checked over the saddle to make sure it was fitted properly. After making a few adjustments, Clint paused before climbing onto Eclipse's back. "Do we leave now, or can we eat first?"

Proffit simply looked over at Clint with the same expression frozen upon his face. The gang leader then looked over to Sonny, who seemed to be wearing the same expression. Then, at the same time, they both broke out into a laugh that seemed to lift some tension without seeming altogether humorous.

"You hear that, Sonny?" Proffit said. "He's about to head out on a ride where hardly any of us may be coming back and he wants to know if he can eat first." Proffit turned to Clint and nodded. "Sure, Matt. Go grab something to eat with the others."

Between the anticipation of the moment which coursed through the air and the bloodthirsty glint in Sonny's eyes, Clint's appetite suddenly seemed to taper off.

FORTY

The meal hall was full to bursting when Clint stepped in
through the double doors. With all the things he had to
think about, what was served to him on a dented tin plate
was the least of them. Looking back on it, he thought it
was oatmeal and corn bread, but he wouldn't have bet on
it. Whatever it was, it was hot, filled his stomach and was
washed down with coffee strong enough to drop a full-
grown bull.

After breakfast, Clint left the hall along with several
others who were all headed in the same direction. Sonny
and Proffit waited outside, both sitting in their saddles as
if they'd been waiting in that very spot since the last time
Clint had seen them.

"All right, all of you," Sonny barked. "Mount up and
be quick about it. We got a long way to ride and a short
time to get there!"

With that, Sonny snapped his own reins and got his
horse running toward the basin's only exit. The rest of
the men jumped onto the backs of their own horses and
scrambled to keep up.

Clint climbed into his own saddle and flicked Eclipse's
reins. Although he wanted to keep up with the party, Clint

didn't want to appear overly anxious. Even though he'd been living the life of an outlaw for a short period of time, he'd picked up on the subtle differences that separated himself from the lawless.

Much like living in a jungle, there was a distinct pecking order as well as ways to behave which a man either took as gospel or died by. When Clint left the persona of Matt Hendershott behind, he knew he would keep part of that outlaw mentality for his own. If anything, it would help him better understand what drove dangerous men.

That kind of knowledge was essential for his way of life, much in the way it was essential for a hunter to know his prey. Of course, he didn't want to get ahead of himself either. Using whatever bits of knowledge he picked up hinged on making it out of Dead End Pass alive.

Clint felt more comfortable letting the rest of the gang ride on ahead so he could keep them all in his sights. One man stayed behind, however, as if he was thinking the same thing.

Jeremiah Proffit sat perched on his horse with one hand across his saddle horn. He watched the rest of the men take off and let his eyes settle on Clint when he saw the Darley Arabian stallion was hanging back. Rather than spur Clint along with words, he rode right up to him and smacked Eclipse on the rump.

"Come on, Matt," Proffit said. "Let's get a move on!"

Clint set a pace that put him directly beside Proffit. It was only then that he saw the second group of men riding out of another exit from the pass. Spotting those other riders, Clint wasn't sure which bothered him more: the fact that the number of robbers had doubled for this trip or that he hadn't seen that whole other group coming.

Proffit was looking over to those others as well. He then looked back to Clint and nodded like a proud general overseeing his troops. "We'll be needing them others,

Matt. And watch where you're riding, by the way. Keep behind the man in front of you."

When Clint steered Eclipse a little over to one side, he saw Proffit nod approvingly.

"I've kept our raiding parties down to eight other men for a reason, you know," Proffit said. "This way, when it counts, they'll only be expecting that many. That is, of course, assuming they even figure we're coming at all."

"If you don't mind me asking," Clint said, "were you planning on telling us where we're going?"

"You're the low man on the totem pole, Hendershott. You should be happy enough that you're coming along at all. But, seeing as how it's too late for you to do anything about it now, I suppose you might as well know the rest. After all, I wouldn't want you to be surprised when you find yourself drawing against federal troops."

"Federal troops?" Clint said, acting as though the possibility had come as a complete surprise.

"Well, they might not be dressed as such, but there'll be soldiers guarding the shipment we're after."

"And what shipment is that? Another of McPike's wagons?"

"Not hardly. Those jobs served their purpose by funding this whole endeavor while also setting us up in the minds of the authorities." Proffit paused for a moment as the entire party rode through a tight canyon leading out into the wider, more well-known trail.

For the next couple of minutes, the thunder of all the horses bounced off the high, rocky walls to assault everyone's ears like the roar of a hurricane. It felt as though Clint's entire head was suddenly filled with rushing water and his skull was being pummeled from the inside. The other men were more used to the stretch of noisy trail and merely pushed on until the walls opened up a bit more around them.

Once he and Clint rode into the more open area, Proffit picked up right where he'd left off. "You were right in thinking that we've been sending messages by being so brutal and letting folks live to tell about it. We're known threats now, but the sweet part of the whole thing is that the law don't know half as much as they think they do.

"They think they know we ride in a gang of nine, but the next time we strike, it'll be double that. Even if they track us, which I doubt they'll be sharp enough to do, they won't know how many of us there are because of our formation. And they won't think twice about that formation, because it's how we've always ridden.

"And best of all, everyone out there who listens to the ones we let go all know about Sonny being the leader of this gang. Not a single one of them knows about me, which will be one hell of a surprise when they find out the hard way."

"So what are we robbing, then?" Clint asked, as if he didn't already have a pretty good idea.

Proffit looked over at him with a beaming smile. "Well, there's already enough money to spread around to make every one of us rich men. Now, what's left is to take the only other thing worth stealing and that's power, Matt. The way this is set up, we'll be able to grab for the reins of this entire state and nobody will be able to stop us."

Hearing that, Clint put on a smile to match Proffit's own. Inside, there was one thing that made Clint's nerves twitch beneath his skin: Proffit was absolutely right.

FORTY-ONE

The gang rode in two separate groups for most of the time. Every so often, both groups would merge into one, but the two row formation was never broken. Clint even looked back every so often to study what he could see of the tracks they'd left behind. It was obvious that the gang had some healthy numbers, but it was next to impossible to tell what that exact number could be.

What frustrated him even more was the fact that most men trying to track the gang would more than likely fall back on what they already knew about its habits. And that, unfortunately, was precisely what Proffit wanted them to do.

Clint tried to think of a way to break off from the group and send out a warning to the governor's office about the impending attack. Only two things kept Clint from doing so: the fact that he was being watched like a hawk and the fact that he didn't have an exact location of where the attack was to take place.

In his time with the gang, Clint had found out a great many things. All of that knowledge still wasn't enough to put a stop to the events that Sonny Byrnes and Jeremiah Proffit had already put into motion. Still, Clint did take some comfort from the knowledge that he'd done the right thing in striking out on his own rather than trying to call in the law right away.

If he'd called in a posse, and even if he'd ridden on the posse himself, Clint would have just sent a lot of good lawmen to their deaths. Proffit was known to be smarter than any of the men who'd tried to bring him down. That was his biggest weapon and it served him better than any firearm.

After stopping to make two separate camps, the entire group of riders settled in for the night just as the last traces of sunlight were fading from the sky. Clint was in the group headed by Proffit; Sonny had taken off to head the second group.

Both teams had camped far enough away from each other so they wouldn't be taken as one splintered group. And even though he couldn't see them from where he was, Clint knew those other men were out there. The governor and soldiers guarding him, on the other hand, had no idea.

In fact, Clint doubted the targets even knew they were in the crosshairs.

Something gnawed in the pit of Clint's stomach, urging him to take action now before it was too late. It was that something which made his thoughts stray constantly back to that town they'd passed a few miles back. Those same thoughts drifted to the telegraph lines that he'd spotted running through that very town.

What wrapped it all up in Clint's mind was the very reason that he'd taken on the name of Matt Hendershott in the first place. He wanted to keep anyone else from being slaughtered by the killers and thieves that had nearly ended Frank Zeller's life. And Clint couldn't save much of anyone if he played it safe and did as he was told by the same killers he meant to stop.

Without saying anything to anyone, Clint walked up to

Eclipse and started strapping the saddle onto the Darley Arabian's back.

"What do you think you're doing?" one of the other gang members asked.

"Just going to get some peace and quiet for a spell. Never you mind."

Before the other man could say a thing, he was stopped by a familiar hand on his shoulder. Proffit moved the other man aside and walked up to Clint.

"You shouldn't go anywhere, Matt," Proffit said. The command in his voice was perfectly clear, as was the subtle threat. "Whatever you need, it's all right here."

Clint looked around to make sure there wasn't anyone else close enough to hear him. "Someone spotted us from that town back there. I figure if I go in, have a drink and let it be known that we're just passing through, it'll keep anyone from paying us any mind."

"Let them think whatever the hell they want. It won't matter."

"Sure it won't. Not until we're through with this and bounty hunters and trackers of all kinds start trying to retrace our steps. Knowing we passed through here is just one more link that'll lead all the way back to Dead End Pass."

Proffit thought that over for a few seconds before narrowing his eyes and studying Clint carefully. "I don't think so. Not alone, anyway."

"Then let someone come along. But I'm telling you, it won't do a bit of good if I ride into town with a known man beside me."

"Makes sense." Proffit nodded, but didn't seem convinced. Before he could say anything else, however, he was interrupted by a voice that came from behind him and to his right.

"I think I need to ride out for a bit, Jer."

Proffit turned to smirk at the youthful face beside him.

"Don't tell me you want to head to town also, Dell."

The kid shrugged and said, "I think I saw someone watching us when we passed it. It wouldn't do to leave behind loose ends now after we been so careful, would it?"

"No, it wouldn't," Proffit said. "All right then, since you two both have the same idea in your heads, then both of you go to town and have your drinks. But if I smell a woman on either of you when you get back, I'll know why you really wanted to ride off on your own and I'll skin you for it."

Watching Proffit smirk at both him and the kid, Clint was reminded of the way a crocodile's mouth appeared to be twisted into a smile right before it clamped down on its meal. Rather than wait for Proffit to change his mind, Clint finished getting Eclipse ready and then climbed into the saddle.

"Hold up there," Proffit said to Dell as he pulled the kid aside. Lowering his voice to a whisper, he said, "Cover our tracks and get a few bottles of whiskey while you're at it."

"Yes, sir," the kid replied.

"And if you see Matt step out of line even by an inch, you know what to do?"

Dell gave one, solemn nod. "Yes, sir. I do."

Proffit stared into the kid's eyes as though he was peering into the younger man's soul. Finally, he slapped Dell on the shoulder and sent him on his way. "Good. I always knew you'd turn out to be one of my favorites."

The kid was fairly beaming with pride when he heard that and rushed to get his own horse ready before Clint was able to ride off without him. He saddled up and flicked his reins just as Eclipse started trotting away from the camp.

Clint couldn't hear much of what was said between Proffit and Dell, but he had a fairly good idea of what it was. He was losing some ground in the gang leader's eyes, but Clint couldn't really help that. He had a job to do that was more important than anything else and he meant to see it through.

Clint was actually impressed with how quickly the kid caught up to him. Apparently, Dell meant to impress his boss by keeping as good an eye on him as he had before. But there was something different in the kid's eyes when Clint looked at him this time.

There was something about the younger man that seemed more intense or more aware. Clint wasn't too happy about either one of those options and hoped that he wasn't forced to do something drastic to keep Dell from becoming too much of a problem.

Then again, judging by the way the kid kept looking at him, Clint figured he wasn't going to have much choice. Trying to keep one eye on the path ahead and the other on the kid riding next to him, Clint snapped his reins and drove onward into the night.

FORTY-TWO

He'd spotted the telegraph office on his way into town. As he passed the darkened little building, Clint's mind raced as he considered how he could get rid of Dell, find the telegraph operator, get the office opened and his message sent, all while trying to appear like he was doing what he told Proffit he was going to do.

Not much had been said on the ride into town between Dell and Clint. In fact, Clint was more nervous about the tense silence than he would have been if the kid had spewed threats at him the entire time. At this point in the game, Clint wanted to know what was going on in every player's mind.

He surely didn't expect to see a gun pointed at him when he turned around to let Dell know that he'd spotted a saloon. Clint pulled Eclipse to a stop and turned so he could face the kid head-on. Dell held his gun with a grip so tight that his knuckles were turning white around the handle.

"What's on your mind, kid?" Clint asked.

Dell swallowed hard and dropped another surprise into Clint's lap. "I know what you did to those two men from the wagon."

"Of course you do. You were there."

"I went back to check on them." Pausing, Dell lowered his eyes, but only for a moment before snapping them back up again. "I wanted to bury them properly, but they weren't there."

"Animals probably dragged them—"

"There were tracks," Dell cut in. "They weren't dead. You didn't kill them like you said you did."

Clint hadn't wanted to hurt Dell. He seemed like a kid with a spark of promise in him and the prospect of where this situation was headed tied Clint's stomach in a knot. "So what did Proffit tell you?" Clint asked. "Take me out here and kill me?"

"Proffit doesn't know what I know. He thinks them guards are dead."

Just when Clint thought he was through with surprises, another one came along to smack him right in the face.

"Proffit's crazy," Dell said after a long, quiet moment had passed. "He and Sonny are both killers. I'm nothing but a thief myself, but I'm no killer. I thought I was sign-ing on to ride with a gang of robbers and I wound up with more blood on my hands than I can live with. And this governor . . ." He let that trail off while shaking his head as though he still couldn't believe what was hap-pening.

"Why did Proffit decide to target a governor and how did he get the information?" Clint asked.

Dell took a deep breath and sat up as though a weight had been taken from his shoulders. Now that he'd com-mitted to his decision, everything that went along with it became much easier to bear. "Like I said, Proffit's crazy. Mr. Conroy knows the governor and Proffit found out what he needed to know from him."

"Does Conroy want this governor harmed?"

"I don't think so. I'm Sonny's nephew, so they all trust me. I hear plenty of things and it sounds like this is all

Proffit's doing. He thinks he can put the fear of God into this governor, collect the ransom and then push the governor around when he gets back into office.

"He says even if he has to kill the governor, he can use his businessmen friends to put up enough money to elect a replacement candidate. Proffit thinks it'll be the next best thing to having the office himself."

Clint had to agree that Proffit wasn't the soundest mind there was. On the other hand, the notion of using crooked politicians to benefit a gang of thugs and killers wasn't half as crazy as Dell thought it to be.

"I came here to stop this," Clint said. "And so did you. Isn't that why you're telling me this now?"

There was a flicker of hope in the kid's eyes, but it was tempered with even more caution. "I do want to stop him, but I ain't sure about you. Maybe you're just as bad as them. Maybe you're worse."

"If I was worse," Clint said, "those two guards would have holes through their heads instead of cuts over their ears."

Dell thought about that for a moment or two, nodded and then holstered his gun. "Why did you want to come into town?"

"To use the telegraph. If we can let somebody know what's coming, we can save that governor's life and put those killers where they belong. If you don't want to cross your uncle, I understand."

"I may share blood with that man, but he would've led me right into an early grave. Just promise me you'll try to see he stays alive."

With everything he knew about Sonny Byrnes, Clint was certain keeping himself alive would be hard enough. Fighting his way through while also trying to keep from killing Sonny in the process would be one hell of an order to fill. Even so, he nodded and said, "I promise to do everything I can to keep from putting Sonny down. I can't guarantee it, though."

"I understand. The sad thing is that at this point, I put more stock in your word than I do my uncle's."

Clint rode up so he was within arm's reach of the kid. He then held out his hand and waited for Dell to shake it. Looking straight into the younger man's eyes, Clint sized him up in a matter of seconds. "There won't be any turning back from this once it gets started. You know that, right?"

"I know. I've been thinkin' it over since I saw them guards' tracks. I've stolen in my life, but I'm still a God-fearing man, Mr. Hendershott. I don't want to kill no more and that's all my uncle and Mister Proffit know how to do."

"Those days are over," Clint assured him. "One way or another, they're over."

"What can I do to help?"

"First, we find the man that runs that telegraph service. Next, we send a message to some of the right people and tell them where they need to be and when they need to get there."

"I'll tell you whatever you need to know."

It was a funny thing. Just when Clint had been getting used to wearing the skin of a snake and slithering in the company of snakes, he was shown that the world wasn't filled with as many snakes as he thought.

FORTY-THREE

With both himself and Dell working on the task, Clint was able to track down the telegraph operator and get his message sent off. Dell had become very quiet, but was more of a help than Clint could have even hoped for. He knew where they were going and when they meant to arrive. In fact, the kid knew so much that Clint had the suspicion there was more than just one figure skulking about the shadows and breaking into lockboxes.

That had all happened two nights ago.

In the time since then, Clint had met back up with the gang and moved along with the group under the leadership of Jeremiah Proffit and Sonny Byrnes. Along the way, Clint had been comparing where they were heading and how fast they were going with what Dell had told him.

It all checked out. Not only that, but Dell hadn't said much of anything to anyone else in the gang apart from returning casual greetings with a wave or nod. Even now, as Proffit's group was brought to a stop in the middle of a wide-open stretch of land, Dell stayed toward the back of the riders. Clint just hoped that the kid's change in attitude wouldn't spark any unwanted suspicion.

That, however, didn't seem like it was going to be a problem. Judging by the hungry look in Proffit's eyes as he stared at a group of two wagons riding a quarter of a mile or so away, he had much more on his plate than an unhappy kid.

"There it is," Proffit said. "Our ticket to all the money and power we can stomach. I want you boys to split up and flank that wagon. Kill anyone who fires a shot against you, but I want that governor alive. You'll recognize him as the old man cowering for his life inside the wagon."

The gunmen around Clint drew their firearms and began to shift anxiously in their saddles. They'd gone from trudging through another long day of riding to being ready and raring to go. There was only a trace of sunlight remaining in the sky, which cast a dark reddish glow on all their faces. The crimson glow made the robbers look as though they'd already been covered with a fine spray of blood.

After glancing over to Clint and giving him one last anticipatory smirk, Proffit raised his gun in the air and shouted, "Charge!"

Like a division of cavalry troops, the robbers snapped their reins and launched all at once into a gallop. Proffit rode toward the front, but was careful to put two of his more anxious men between himself and the first volley of gunfire. Clint stuck toward the middle of the group while Dell hung all the way back. The kid was still reluctant, but he rode on for the sake of keeping up appearances.

Even though he knew he wasn't a genuine part of the raiding party, Clint could still feel the rush of blood through his veins and the thunder of the charging horses throughout his entire body. The exhilaration was genuine enough and he couldn't help but let out a few hollers of his own to mingle with the ruckus kicked up by the rest of the group. In what felt like the blink of an eye, they'd

closed nearly all the distance between the robbers and
their intended prey.

What separated himself from the others took place
once the first shot was fired. The group had just gotten to
within rifle range when a crack of gunfire and puff of
smoke came from the top of the lead wagon. A round
hissed through the air and slapped directly into the chest
of the robber at the front of the group.

That man wavered and then dropped from his saddle,
causing the horse behind him to act on reflex and jump
over his rolling body. The next horse wasn't so quick,
however, and turned the fallen man's ribs into powder
with one solid kick. When Clint checked behind him, he
saw nothing but a crumpled form in the dirt that could
barely pass for human.

"Fire!" Proffit screamed.

The gunmen around Proffit started pulling their triggers, adding the roar of blazing six-guns to the pounding
chaos of all those horses running at top speed. Men from
the wagon were shooting back as well, but were missing
more than hitting since they were now under heavy fire.

As far as Clint could tell, one of the men nearby had
been wounded, but was still pulling his trigger. While he
was taking stock of the robbers, Clint saw another one
catch a bullet from the wagon in his left eye. The impact
from the flying lead snapped his head back and to one
side, pulling the rest of his body completely off the back
of his horse.

The riders were closing in on the wagon fast. Soon,
Clint knew the wagon would be well within the range of
all the robbers' pistols. Once that happened, the men in
those two wagons were in serious trouble.

As if sensing the thoughts racing through Clint's mind,
Proffit turned around to check in on him. "Circle around
that second wagon, Matt. Take Dell with you. Me and the

rest will—" But Proffit stopped before finishing his orders.

He stopped because Matt Hendershott was no longer looking back at him. Instead, there was a clarity in the other man's eyes that hadn't quite been there before. There was even something different about his voice.

"Call this off, Proffit," Clint said. It seemed so long since he'd spoken in his own natural voice that it rang loud and clear even over the roar of hooves and gunfire. "This is your only chance."

Proffit's eyes widened and his mouth hung open. At that moment, he didn't seem to notice or even care about the bullets whipping past his head. All he saw was the gun being pointed toward him and the steely glint in Clint's eyes.

"Kill this rat son of a bitch!" Proffit shouted to anyone who could hear him.

Several of Proffit's gunmen had already circled around the front of the lead wagon leaving Clint, Dell and Proffit in the company of just two others. One of those two remaining robbers was wounded and the other looked confused—but he wasn't too confused to mistake the order he'd been given and swing his gun around to point it at Clint.

Although he could only see the other gunman from the corner of his eye, Clint snapped his Colt to that side and took a quick shot. His round clipped the gunman in the upper torso and yanked him back as though the robber had ridden into an invisible branch.

They were coming up to the wagon now, so rather than risk taking some fire from the soldiers on board, Clint sped ahead and steered Eclipse ninety degrees to the left which brought him directly in Proffit's path. Proffit's horse reared, but the gang leader hung on. When the animal steadied itself once again, Proffit was staring up close into Clint's eyes.

Clint swung his gun arm straight out, smashing the Colt's handle into Proffit's nose. Rather than retaliate with his fist, the gang leader aimed his pistol at Clint and squeezed the trigger.

The gun barked once and Clint felt a burning pain slice through his right side. Once the initial round of pain wore off, he was left with a slight light-headed feeling, but nothing more than that. It was a flesh wound. Even with that good fortune, Clint wasn't about to sit back and count his blessings just yet.

Men were falling all around him. One or two were unfamiliar soldiers, but one of them Clint recognized as a robber from his group. When he glanced over again to see what the man was doing, he found nothing but a riderless horse. Not far from where the gunman had been, Dell was riding with a smoking gun clutched in his hand.

So far, the wagons had taken their losses but were still going strong. Before Clint could feel too happy about that, he saw something that made his spirits drop: the second group of robbers led by Sonny Byrnes.

Those men were thundering toward them and had already started shooting. Worse than that, Sonny himself had just put a bullet through the skull of the lead wagon's driver.

FORTY-FOUR

Proffit's face was a bloody mess, but he was far from out of the fight. As Clint touched his heels to Eclipse's sides, he saw Proffit take aim at him and squeeze off a round. The bullet went high and Clint had no choice but to let it go unanswered. He knew that if he didn't get control of that wagon, then Sonny or one of his men would get hold of those reins.

Another shot came from behind Clint, followed by a pained grunt and the sickening sound of a body slamming into the ground. Clint pushed all that aside and concentrated on steering Eclipse alongside the speeding wagon.

Between all the shouting and shooting, the horses pulling the wagons had been whipped into something close to a frenzy. Even Eclipse had a difficult time matching their speed and pulling up close without being knocked aside, but the Darley Arabian managed to pull it off.

Another shot whipped by Clint's head, this time coming so close that he could almost smell the heated lead. Without letting himself be distracted by the blood that was spilling all around him, the pain coursing through his own body, or even the guns being pointed at him at that very

181

second, Clint swung one leg over Eclipse's back and pushed off with his other.

He reached out with his free hand while twisting his body around in mid-air. Although he was only flying for less than a second, Clint felt as though he'd taken one step too many off the side of a cliff. His free hand desperately took hold of the driver's seat, both feet slammed into the side of the wagon and his body soon followed.

The instant Clint could look around, he spotted Proffit getting ready to take one more shot at him. Clint crouched down in the wagon, lifted his Colt and aimed it as if he was simply pointing his finger and then took his shot. The Colt spat out its round and knocked Proffit backwards in his saddle. Clint sprang back up to look at his target.

There was a crazy fire in Proffit's eyes which seemed even more hellish given the fact that there was a gaping hole over his right brow. It was the gang leader's last effort to lift his gun and take another shot at Clint, but even that was denied him. Clint fired another shot into Proffit's chest. This time, not only did it finish the killer for good, but it knocked him clean off the backside of his horse.

Clint didn't have time to worry about the rest of the gang because he needed to slow the wagon before the horses were too far out of control. He pulled back on the reins and leaned over to a wounded man who'd been riding shotgun.

"Is the governor all right?" Clint asked.

The guard blinked a few times and started scrambling for the holdout pistol at his hip.

"My name's Clint Adams. I sent you a warning that this would happen. Did you get it?"

"That . . . that was you?" The guard was fighting to stay awake after losing so much blood, but he was able to pull himself together. "Yeah, we got the message. The governor is locked up tight inside the wagon."

"Is that the only precaution you took?"

"No . . . it isn't. They're just a bit late, that's all."

"Who's late?"

The guard nodded toward the direction where Sonny and his group were thundering toward the wagon. "They are, but they're here now."

Finally, Clint spotted who the guard was really talking about. Behind the approaching gang of robbers, there was another group of men on horseback. Not only did that other group outnumber the robbers three to one, but they were armed with rifles and wearing U.S. Cavalry uniforms.

As Clint watched, the cavalry riders let loose with their first round of gunfire. If Sonny or any of his men had realized there was anyone behind them, it was too late for them to do anything about it now. Several of the robbers went down as either they or their horses caught a sudden, and very painful, dose of lead.

Clint was able to bring the wagon to a stop and Eclipse was right there when he did. A few of the nearby gunmen were still trying to do some damage, but Clint picked them off before they could hit anyone else in or on the wagons.

In the distance, the crackle of gunfire went on like a string of fireworks, punctuated by the barking commands of the cavalry officers for the robbers to surrender. Clint was just about to climb back into his own saddle when he heard a familiar voice shout a familiar name.

"Matt Hendershott!" Sonny Byrnes shouted. "You're a dead man!"

Clint could see the blood soaked into the gang leader's clothes and the crazy fire in his eyes even from the distance of over fifty yards away. He could also see the cavalry riders closing in on Sonny, who was the last man left alive of his entire group.

"Throw your hands up and surrender," one of the cavalry ordered.

Sonny gave Clint one more hateful look before lifting his gun to take a shot at the soldiers who'd closed in around him. In the next split second, the mounted soldiers pulled their triggers, gunning Sonny Byrnes down like he was a man propped in front of a firing squad.

Clint looked over to Dell who'd tossed his gun, dismounted and was surrendering to one of the men guarding the governor.

"I'm sorry, kid."